OCTOPUSSY, THE DARLING,

was a bit surly. The tentacle she lashed around Major Smythe's arm that ___ ing was none too gentle. So w___ ___ d himself the sudd___ ___ND at cocktail t___ ___nt, if rather grue___

THE LIVING ___GHTS

are about to be blasted out of a living target on a crowded Berlin street. Crouched behind a .308 International Experimental Target rifle, JAMES BOND sights his victim, makes a split-second decision, and gently squeezes the trigger . . .

THE PROPERTY OF A LADY,

a valuable objet d'art, is about to be auctioned at Sotheby's. At the start of the bargaining, the room becomes electric with danger and terror, and nobody but JAMES BOND knows why . . .

"[these stories] possess those properties which made the late author's novels so readable—imagination, pace, coolness, and that weave of real or counterfeit fact into the story's very movement, which Kingsley Amis called 'the Fleming effect.' For the 007 faithful, that is enough."—Ed Kelly,

BUFFALO EVENING NEWS

The Best in Fiction from SIGNET

(0451)

OCTOPUSSY

The Last Great Adventures of James Bond 007

Ian Fleming

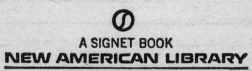

A SIGNET BOOK
NEW AMERICAN LIBRARY

TIMES MIRROR

SIGNET TRADEMARK REG. U.S. PAT. OFF. AND FOREIGN COUNTRIES
REGISTERED TRADEMARK—MARCA REGISTRADA
HECHO EN CHICAGO, U.S.A.

SIGNET, SIGNET CLASSICS, MENTOR, PLUME, MERIDIAN AND NAL
BOOKS *are published by The New American Library, Inc.,*
1633 Broadway, New York, New York 10019

First Printing, July, 1967

5   6   7   8   9   10

PRINTED IN THE UNITED STATES OF AMERICA

CONTENTS

OCTOPUSSY

give us twenty-five years of the good life, just cutting

something, and it took Major Smythe a full year of

Y ou know what?" said Major Dexter Smythe to the octopus. "You're going to have a real treat today if I can manage it."

He had spoken aloud, and his breath had steamed up the glass of his Pirelli mask. He put his feet down to the sand beside the coral boulder and stood up. The water reached to his armpits. He took off the mask and spat into it, rubbed the spit round the glass, rinsed it clean, and pulled the rubber band of the mask back over his head. He bent down again.

The eye in the mottled brown sack was still watching him carefully from the hole in the coral, but now the tip of a single small tentacle wavered hesitatingly an inch or two out of the shadows and quested vaguely with its pink suckers uppermost. Dexter Smythe smiled with satisfaction. Given time—perhaps one more month on top of the two during which he had been chumming the octopus—and he would have tamed

the darling. But he wasn't going to have that month.
Should he take a chance today and reach down and
offer his hand, instead of the expected lump of raw
meat on the end of his spear, to the tentacle? Shake
it by the hand, so to speak? No, Pussy, he thought. I
can't quite trust you yet. Almost certainly other
tentacles would whip out of the hole and up his arm.
He only needed to be dragged down less than two feet
for the cork valve on his mask to automatically close,
and he would be suffocated inside it or, if he tore it
off, drowned. He might get in a quick lucky jab with
his spear, but it would take more than that to kill
Pussy. No. Perhaps later in the day. It would be rather
like playing Russian roulette, and at about the same
five-to-one odds. It might be a quick, a whimsical, way
out of his troubles! But not now. It would leave the
interesting question unsolved. And he had promised
that nice Professor Bengry at the Institute. . . . Dexter
Smythe swam leisurely off toward the reef, his eyes
questing for one shape only, the squat, sinister wedge
of a scorpionfish, or, as Bengry would put it, *Scor-
paena plumieri*.

Major Dexter Smythe, O.B.E., Royal Marines
(Retd.), was the remains of a once brave and re-
sourceful officer and of a handsome man who had
had the sexual run of his teeth all his life, particularly
among the Wrens and Wracs and ATS who manned
the communications and secretariat of the very special
task force to which he had been attached at the end
of his service career. Now he was fifty-four and slightly
bald, and his belly sagged in his Jantzen trunks. And
he had had two coronary thromboses, the second (the
"second warning" as his doctor, Jimmy Greaves, who

had been one of their high poker game at Prince's
Club when Dexter Smythe had first come to Jamaica,
had half jocularly put it) only a month before. But,
in his well-chosen clothes, with his varicose veins out
of sight, and with his stomach flattened by a discreet
support belt behind an immaculate cummerbund, he
was still a fine figure of a man at a cocktail party or
dinner on the North Shore. And it was a mystery to
his friends and neighbors why, in defiance of the two
ounces of whiskey and the ten cigarettes a day to which
his doctor had rationed him, he persisted in smoking
like a chimney and going to bed drunk, if amiably
drunk, every night.

The truth of the matter was that Dexter Smythe
had arrived at the frontier of the death wish. The
origins of this state of mind were many and not all
that complex. He was irretrievably tied to Jamaica,
and tropical sloth had gradually riddled him so that,
while outwardly he appeared a piece of fairly solid
hardwood, inside the varnished surface, the termites
of sloth, self-indulgence, guilt over an ancient sin,
and general disgust with himself had eroded his once
hard core into dust. Since the death of Mary two
years before, he had loved no one. (He wasn't even
sure that he had really loved her, but he knew that,
every hour of the day, he missed her love of him and
her gay, untidy, chiding, and often irritating pres-
ence.) And though he ate their canapés and drank
their martinis, he had nothing but contempt for the
international riffraff with whom he consorted on the
North Shore. He could perhaps have made friends
with the more solid elements—the gentleman-farmers
inland, the plantation owners on the coast, the pro-

fessional men, the politicians—but that would mean regaining some serious purpose in life which his sloth, his spiritual accidie, prevented, and cutting down on the bottle, which he was definitely unwilling to do. So Major Smythe was bored, bored to death, and, but for one factor in his life, he would long ago have swallowed the bottle of barbiturates he had easily acquired from a local doctor. The lifeline that kept him clinging to the edge of the cliff was a tenuous one. Heavy drinkers veer toward an exaggeration of their basic temperaments, the classic four—sanguine, phlegmatic, choleric, and melancholic. The sanguine drunk goes gay to the point of hysteria and idiocy; the phlegmatic sinks into a morass of sullen gloom; the choleric is the fighting drunk of the cartoonists who spends much of his life in prison for smashing people and things; and the melancholic succumbs to self-pity, mawkishness, and tears. Major Smythe was a melancholic who had slid into a drooling fantasy woven around the birds and insects and fish that inhabited the five acres of Wavelets (the name he had given his small villa was symptomatic), its beach, and the coral reef beyond. The fish were his particular favorites. He referred to them as "people," and since reef fish stick to their territories as closely as do most small birds, he knew them all, after two years, intimately, "loved" them, and believed that they loved him in return.

They certainly knew him, as the denizens of zoos know their keepers, because he was a daily and a regular provider, scraping off algae and stirring up the sand and rocks for the bottom-feeders, breaking up sea eggs and sea urchins for the small carnivores, and bringing out scraps of offal for the larger ones. And now, as he swam slowly and heavily up and down the reef and through the channels that led out to deep water, his "people" swarmed around him fearlessly and expectantly, darting at the tip of the three-pronged spear they knew only as a prodigal spoon, flirting right up to the glass of the Pirelli, and even, in the case of the fearless, pugnacious demoiselles, nipping softly at his feet and legs.

Part of Major Smythe's mind took in all these brilliantly colored little "people" and he greeted them in unspoken words. ("Morning, Beau Gregory" to the dark blue demoiselle sprinkled with bright blue spots—the jewelfish that exactly resembles the starlit fashioning of a bottle of Guerlain's Dans La Nuit; "Sorry. Not today, sweetheart" to a fluttering butterflyfish with false black eyes on its tail; and "You're too fat anyway, Blue Boy," to an indigo parrotfish that must have weighed a good ten pounds.) But today he had a job to do and his eyes were searching for only one of his "people"—his only enemy on the reef, the only one he killed on sight, a scorpionfish.

The scorpionfish inhabits most of the southern waters of the world, and the rascasse that is the foundation of bouillabaisse belongs to the family. The West Indian variety runs up to only about twelve inches long and perhaps a pound in weight. It is by far the ugliest fish in the sea, as if nature were giving warning. It is a mottled brownish gray with a heavy wedge-shaped shaggy head. It has fleshy pendulous "eyebrows" that droop over angry red eyes and a coloration and broken silhouette that are perfect camouflage on the reef. Though a small fish, its heavily toothed mouth is so wide that it can swallow whole

most of the smaller reef fishes, but its supreme weapon
lies in its erectile dorsal fins, the first few of which,
acting on contact like hypodermic needles, are fed by
poison glands containing enough dotoxin to kill a
man if they merely graze him in a vulnerable spot—in
an artery, for instance, or over the heart or in the
groin. It constitutes the only real danger to the reef
swimmer, far more dangerous than the barracuda or
the shark, because, supreme in its confidence in its
camouflage and armory, it flees before nothing except
the very close approach of a foot or actual contact.
Then it flits only a few yards, on wide and bizarrely
striped pectorals, and settles again watchfully either
on the sand, where it looks like a lump of overgrown
coral, or among the rocks and seaweed where it vir-
tually disappears. And Major Smythe was determined
to find one and spear it and give it to his octopus to
see if it would take it or spurn it—to see if one of the
ocean's great predators would recognize the deadliness
of another, know of its poison. Would the octopus
consume the belly and leave the spines? Would it eat
the lot? And if so, would it suffer from the poison?
These were the questions Bengry at the Institute
wanted answered, and today, since it was going to be
the beginning of the end of Major Smythe's life at
Wavelets—and though it might mean the end of his
darling Octopussy—Major Smythe had decided to find
out the answers and leave one tiny memorial to his
now futile life in some dusty corner of the Institute's
marine biological files.

For, in only the last couple of hours, Major Dexter
Smythe's already dismal life had changed very much
for the worse. So much for the worse that he would

be lucky if, in a few weeks' time—time for an exchange of cables via Government House and the Colonial Office to the Secret Service and thence to Scotland Yard and the Public Prosecutor, and for Major Smythe's transportation to London with a police escort—he got away with a sentence of imprisonment for life.

And all this because of a man called Bond, Commander James Bond, who had turned up at ten-thirty that morning in a taxi from Kingston.

The day had started normally. Major Smythe had awakened from his Seconal sleep, swallowed a couple of Panadols (his heart condition forbade him aspirin), showered, skimped his breakfast under the umbrella-shaped sea almonds, and spent an hour feeding the remains of his breakfast to the birds. He then took his prescribed doses of anticoagulant and blood-pressure pills and killed time with the *Daily Gleaner* until it was time for his elevenses, which, for some months now, he had advanced to ten-thirty. He had just poured himself the first of two stiff brandy and ginger ales (The Drunkard's Drink) when he heard the car coming up the drive.

Luna, his colored housekeeper, came out into the garden and announced "Gemmun to see you, Major."

"What's his name?"

"Him doan say, Major. Him say to tell you him come from Govment House."

Major Smythe was wearing nothing but a pair of old khaki shorts and sandals. He said, "All right, Luna. Put him in the living room and say I won't be

a moment." And he went round the back way into
his bedroom and put on a white bush shirt and trousers and brushed his hair. Government House! Now
what the hell?

As soon as he had walked through into the living
room and seen the tall man in the dark blue tropical
suit standing at the picture window looking out to
sea, Major Smythe had somehow sensed bad news.
And, when the man had turned slowly toward him
and looked at him with watchful, serious gray-blue
eyes, he had known that this was officialdom, and
when his cheery smile was not returned, inimical
officialdom. And a chill had run down Major Smythe's
spine. "They" had somehow found out.

"Well, well. I'm Smythe. I gather you're from Government House. How's Sir Kenneth?"

There was somehow no question of shaking hands.
The man said, "I haven't met him. I only arrived a
couple of days ago. I've been out round the island
most of the time. My name's Bond, James Bond. I'm
from the Ministry of Defense."

Major Smythe remembered the hoary euphemism
for the Secret Service. He said bonhomously, "Oh.
The old firm?"

The question had been ignored. "Is there somewhere we can talk?"

"Rather. Anywhere you like. Here or in the garden? What about a drink?" Major Smythe clinked
the ice in the glass he still held in his hand. "Rum
and ginger's the local poison. I prefer the ginger by
itself." The lie came out with the automatic smooth-
ness of the alcoholic.

"No thanks. And here would be fine." The man

leaned negligently against the wide mahogany windowsill.

Major Smythe sat down and threw a jaunty leg over the low arm of one of the comfortable planters' chairs he had had copied from an original by the local cabinetmaker. He pulled out the drink coaster from the other arm, took a deep pull at his glass, and slid it, with a consciously steady hand, down into the hole in the wood. "Well," he said cheerily, looking the other man straight in the eyes, "what can I do for you? Somebody been up to some dirty work on the North Shore and you need a spare hand? Be glad to get into harness again. It's been a long time since those days, but I can still remember some of the old routines."

"Do you mind if I smoke?" The man had already got his cigarette case in his hand. It was a flat gunmetal one that would hold around twenty-five. Somehow this small sign of a shared weakness comforted Major Smythe.

"Of course, my dear fellow." He made a move to get up, his lighter ready.

"It's all right, thanks." James Bond had already lit his cigarette. "No, it's nothing local. I want to . . . I've been sent out to . . . ask you to recall your work for the Service at the end of the war." James Bond paused and looked down at Major Smythe carefully. "Particularly the time when you were working with the Miscellaneous Objectives Bureau."

Major Smythe laughed sharply. He had known it. He had known it for absolutely sure. But when it came out of this man's mouth, the laugh had been forced out of Major Smythe like the scream of a hit man. "Oh Lord, yes. Good old MOB. That was a lark all right." He laughed again. He felt the anginal pain, brought on by the pressure of what he knew was coming, build up across his chest. He dipped his hand into his trouser pocket, tilted the little bottle into the palm of his hand, and slipped the white TNT pill under his tongue. He was amused to see the tension coil up in the other man, the way the eyes narrowed watchfully. *It's all right, my dear fellow. This isn't a death pill.* He said, "You troubled with acidosis? No? It slays me when I go on a bender. Last night. Party at Jamaica Inn. One really ought to stop thinking one's always twenty-five. Anyway, let's get back to MOB Force. Not many of us left, I suppose." He felt the pain across his chest withdraw into its lair. "Something to do with the Official History?"

James Bond looked down at the tip of his cigarette. "Not exactly."

"I expect you know I wrote most of the chapter on the Force for the War Book. It's fifteen years since then. Doubt if I'd have much to add today."

"Nothing more about that operation in the Tirol —place called Oberaurach, about a mile east of Kitzbühel?"

One of the names he had been living with for fifteen years forced another harsh laugh out of Major Smythe. "That was a piece of cake! You've never seen such a shambles. All those Gestapo toughs with their doxies. All of 'em hog-drunk. They'd kept their files all ticketty-boo. Handed them over without a murmur. Hoped that'd earn 'em easy treatment I suppose. We gave the stuff a first going-over and shipped all the bods off to the Munich camp. Last I heard of them. Most of them hanged for war crimes I expect. We handed the bumf over to HQ at Salzburg. Then we went on up the Mittersill valley after another hideout." Major Smythe took a good pull at his drink and lit a cigarette. He looked up. "That's the long and the short of it."

"You were Number Two at the time, I think. The CO was an American, a Colonel King from Patton's army."

"That's right. Nice fellow. Wore a mustache, which isn't like an American. Knew his way among the local wines. Quite a civilized chap."

"In his report about the operation he wrote that he handed you all the documents for a preliminary run-through as you were the German expert with the unit. Then you gave them all back to him with your comments?" James Bond paused. "Every single one of them?"

Major Smythe ignored the innuendo. "That's right. Mostly lists of names. Counterintelligence dope. The CI people in Salzburg were very pleased with the stuff. Gave them plenty of new leads. I expect the originals are lying about somewhere. They'll have been used for the Nuremberg Trials. Yes, by Jove!"—Major Smythe was reminiscent, pally—"those were some of the jolliest months of my life, haring around the country with MOB Force. Wine, women, and song! And you can say that again!"

Here, Major Smythe was saying the whole truth. He had had a dangerous and uncomfortable war until 1945. When the commandos were formed in 1941, he had volunteered and been seconded from the Royal Marines to Combined Operations Headquarters under

Mountbatten. There his excellent German (his mother
had come from Heidelberg) had earned him the un-
enviable job of being advanced interrogator on com-
mando operations across the Channel. He had been
lucky to get away from two years of this work un-
scathed and with the O.B.E. (Military), which was
sparingly awarded in the last war. And then, in
preparation for the defeat of Germany, the Miscellaneous Objectives Bureau had been formed jointly by
the Secret Service and Combined Operations, and
Major Smythe had been given the temporary rank of
lieutenant colonel and told to form a unit whose job
would be the cleaning up of Gestapo and Abwehr
hideouts when the collapse of Germany came about.
The OSS got to hear of the scheme and insisted on
getting into the act to cope with the American wing of
the front, and the result was the creation of not one
but six units that went into operation in Germany and
Austria on the day of surrender. They were units of
twenty men, each with a light armored car, six jeeps,
a wireless truck, and three lorries, and they were controlled by a joint Anglo-American headquarters in
SHAEF, which also fed them with targets from the
Army Intelligence units and from the SIS and OSS.
Major Smythe had been Number Two of "A" Force,
which had been allotted the Tirol—an area full of
good hiding places with easy access to Italy and perhaps out of Europe—that was known to have been
chosen as funkhole Number One by the people MOB
Force was after. And, as Major Smythe had just told
Bond, they had had themselves a ball. All without firing a shot—except, that is, two fired by Major Smythe.

James Bond said casually, "Does the name of Hannes Oberhauser ring a bell?"

Major Smythe frowned, trying to remember. "Can't say it does." It was eighty degrees in the shade, but he shivered.

"Let me refresh your memory. On the same day as those documents were given to you to look over, you made inquiries at the Tiefenbrünner Hotel, where you were billeted, for the best mountain guide in Kitzbühel. You were referred to Oberhauser. The next day you asked your CO for a day's leave, which was granted. Early next morning you went to Oberhauser's chalet, put him under close arrest, and drove him away in your jeep. Does that ring a bell?"

That phrase about "refreshing your memory." How often had Major Symthe himself used it when he was trying to trap a German liar? *Take your time! You've been ready for something like this for years*. Major Smythe shook his head doubtfully. "Can't say it does."

"A man with graying hair and a gammy leg. Spoke some English, he'd been a ski teacher before the war."

Major Smythe looked candidly into the cold, clear blue eyes. "Sorry. Can't help you."

James Bond took a small blue leather notebook out of his inside pocket and turned the leaves. He stopped turning them. He looked up. "At that time, as side arms, you were carrying a regulation Webley-Scott forty-five with the serial number eight-nine-six-seven-three-sixty-two."

"It was certainly a Webley. Damned clumsy weapon. Hope they've got something more like the

Luger or the heavy Beretta these days. But I can't say
I ever took a note of the number."

"The number's right enough," said James Bond.
"I've got the date of its issue to you by HQ and the
date when you turned it in. You signed the book both
times."

Major Smythe shrugged. "Well then, it must have
been my gun. But"—he put rather angry impatience
into his voice—"what, if I may ask, is all this in aid
of?"

James Bond looked at him almost with curiosity.
He said, and now his voice was not unkind, "You
know what it is all about, Smythe." He paused and
seemed to reflect. "Tell you what. I'll go out into
the garden for ten minutes or so. Give you time to
think things over. Give me a hail." He added seriously
"It'll make things so much easier for you if you come
out with the story in your own words."

Bond walked to the door into the garden. He turned
around. "I'm afraid it's only a question of dotting the
i's and crossing the *t*'s. You see I had a talk with the
Foo brothers in Kingston yesterday." He stepped out
onto the lawn.

Something in Major Smythe was relieved. Now at
least the battle of wits, the trying to invent alibis, the
evasions, were over. If this man Bond had got to the
Foos, to either of them, they would have spilled the
beans. The last thing they wanted was to get in bad
with the government, and anyway there was only about
six inches of the stuff left.

Major Smythe got briskly to his feet and went to
the loaded sideboard and poured himself out another
brandy and ginger ale, almost fifty-fifty. He might as

well live it up while there was still time! The future
wouldn't hold many more of these for him. He went
back to his chair and lit his twentieth cigarette of the
day. He looked at his watch. It said eleven-thirty. If
he could be rid of the chap in an hour, he'd have
plenty of time with his "people." He sat and drank and
marshaled his thoughts. He could make the story long
or short, put in the weather and the way the flowers
and pines had smelled on the mountain, or he could
cut it short. He would cut it short.

Up in that big double bedroom in the Tiefenbrünner, with the wads of buff and gray paper spread
out on the spare bed, he hadn't been looking for anything special, just taking samples here and there and
concentrating on the ones marked, in red, KOM-
MANDOSACHE—HÖCHST VERTRAULICH. There weren't
many of these, and they were mostly confidential re-
ports on German top brass, intercepts of broken allied
ciphers, and information about the whereabouts of
secret dumps. Since these were the main targets of
"A" Force, Major Smythe had scanned them with
particular excitement—food, explosives, guns, espionage records, files of Gestapo personnel. A tremendous
haul! And then, at the bottom of the packet, there
had been the single envelope sealed with red wax
and the notation ONLY TO BE OPENED IN FINAL
EMERGENCY. The envelope contained one single sheet
of paper. It was unsigned, and the few words were
written in red ink. The heading said VALUTA, and beneath it was written: WILDE KAISER. FRANZISKANER
HALT. 100 M. ÖSTLICH STEINHÜGEL. WAFFENKISTE.
ZWEI BAR 24 KT. Under that was a list of measure-

ments in centimeters. Major Smythe held his hands apart as if telling a story about a fish he had caught. The bars would be about as wide as his shoulders and about two by four inches. And one single English sovereign of only eighteen carats was selling nowadays for two to three pounds! This was a bloody fortune! Forty, fifty thousand pounds worth! Maybe even a hundred! He didn't stop to think, but, quite coolly and speedily, in case anyone should come in, he put a match to the paper and the envelope, ground the ashes to powder, and swilled them down the lavatory. Then he took out his large-scale Austrian ordnance map of the area and in a moment had his finger on the Franziskaner Halt. It was marked as an uninhabited mountaineer's refuge on a saddle just below the highest of the easterly peaks of the Kaiser mountains, that awe-inspiring range of giant stone teeth that gave Kitzbühel its threatening northern horizon. And the cairn of stones would be about there—his fingernail pointed—and the whole bloody lot was only ten miles and perhaps a five hours' climb away!

The beginning had been as this fellow Bond had described. He had gone to Oberhauser's chalet at four in the morning, had arrested him, and had told his weeping, protesting family that Smythe was taking him to an interrogation camp in Munich. If the guide's record was clean he would be back home within a week. If the family kicked up a fuss it would only make trouble for Oberhauser. Smythe had refused to give his name and had had the forethought to shroud the numbers on his jeep. In twenty-four hours, "A" Force would be on its way, and by the time military government got to Kitzbühel, the incident would already be buried under the morass of the Occupation tangle.

Oberhauser had been a nice enough chap once he had recovered from his fright, and when Smythe talked knowingly about skiing and climbing, both of which he had done before the war, the pair, as Smythe intended, became quite pally. Their route lay along the bottom of the Kaiser range to Kufstein, and Smythe drove slowly, making admiring comments on the peaks that were now flushed with the pink of dawn. Finally, below the peak of gold, as he called it to himself, he slowed to a halt and pulled off the road into a grassy glade. He turned in his seat and said with an assumption of candor, "Oberhauser, you are a man after my own heart. We share many interests together, and from your talk, and from the man I think you to be, I am sure you did not cooperate with the Nazis. Now I will tell you what I will do. We will spend the day climbing on the Kaiser, and I will then drive you back to Kitzbühel and report to my commanding officer that you have been cleared at Munich." He grinned cheerfully. "Now. How about that?"

The man had been near to tears of gratitude. But could he have some kind of paper to show that he was a good citizen? Certainly. Major Smythe's signature would be quite enough. The pact was made, the jeep was driven up a track and well hidden from the road, and they were off at a steady pace, climbing up through the pine-scented foothills.

Smythe was well dressed for the climb. He had nothing on except his bush shirt, shorts, and a pair of the excellent rubber-soled boots issued to American parachutists. His only burden was the Webley-Scott, and, tactfully, for Oberhauser was after all one of the enemy, Oberhauser didn't suggest that he leave it behind some conspicuous rock. Oberhauser was in his best suit and boots, but that didn't seem to bother him, and he assured Major Smythe that ropes and pitons would not be needed for their climb and that there was a hut directly up above them where they could rest. It was called the Franziskaner Halt.

"Is it indeed?" said Major Smythe.

"Yes, and below it there is a small glacier. Very pretty, but we will climb round it. There are many crevasses."

"Is that so?" said Major Smythe thoughtfully. He examined the back of Oberhauser's head, now beaded with sweat. After all, he was only a bloody kraut, or at any rate of that ilk. What would one more or less matter? It was all going to be as easy as falling off a log. The only thing that worried Major Smythe was getting the bloody stuff down the mountain. He decided that he would somehow sling the bars across his back. After all, he could slide it most of the way in its ammunition box or whatnot.

It was a long, dreary hack up the mountain, and when they were above the treeline, the sun came up and it was very hot. And now it was all rock and scree, and their long zigzags sent boulders and rubble rumbling and crashing down the slope that got ever steeper as they approached the final crag, gray and menacing, that lanced away into the blue above them. They were both naked to the waist and sweating, so that the sweat ran down their legs into their boots, but despite Oberhauser's limp, they kept up a good pace, and when they stopped for a drink and a

swabdown at a hurtling mountain stream, Oberhauser
congratulated Major Smythe on his fitness. Major
Smythe, his mind full of dreams, said curtly and un-
truthfully that all English soldiers were fit, and they
went on.

The rock face wasn't difficult. Major Smythe had
known that it wouldn't be or the climbers' hut couldn't
have been built on the shoulder. Toeholds had been
cut in the face, and there were occasional iron pegs
hammered into crevices. But he couldn't have found
the more difficult traverses by himself, and he congratulated himself on deciding to bring a guide.

Once, Oberhauser's hand, testing for a grip, dis-
lodged a great slab of rock, loosened by five years of
snow and frost, and sent it crashing down the mountain. Major Smythe suddenly thought about noise.
"Many people around here?" he asked as they watched
the boulder hurtle down into the treeline.

"Not a soul until you get near Kufstein," said
Oberhauser. He gestured along the arid range of high
peaks. "No grazing. Little water. Only the climbers
come here. And since the beginning of the war. . . ."
He left the phrase unfinished.

They skirted the blue-fanged glacier below the
final climb to the shoulder. Major Smythe's careful
eyes took in the width and depth of the crevasses.
Yes, they would fit! Directly above them, perhaps a
hundred feet up under the lee of the shoulder, were
the weatherbeaten boards of the hut. Major Smythe
measured the angle of the slope. Yes, it was almost a
straight dive down. Now or later? He guessed later.
The line of the last traverse wasn't very clear.

They were up at the hut in five hours flat. Major

Smythe said he wanted to relieve himself and wandered casually along the shoulder to the east, paying no heed to the beautiful panoramas of Austria and Bavaria that stretched away on either side of him perhaps fifty miles into the heat haze. He counted his paces carefully. At exactly one hundred and twenty there was the cairn of stones, a loving memorial perhaps to some long dead climber. Major Smythe, knowing differently, longed to tear it apart there and then. Instead he took out his Webley-Scott, squinted down the barrel, and twirled the cylinder. Then he walked back.

It was cold up there at ten thousand feet or more, and Oberhauser had got into the hut and was busy preparing a fire. Major Smythe controlled his horror at the sight. "Oberhauser," he said cheerfully, "come out and show me some of the sights. Wonderful view up here."

"Certainly, Major." Oberhauser followed Major Smythe out of the hut. Outside, he fished in his hip pocket and produced something wrapped in paper. He undid the paper to reveal a hard wrinkled sausage. He offered it to the major. "It is only what we call a *Soldat*," he said shyly. "Smoked meat. Very tough but good." He smiled. "It is like what they eat in Wild West films. What is the name?"

"Pemmican," said the major. Then—and later this had slightly disgusted him with himself—he said, "Leave it in the hut. We will share it later. Come over here. Can we see Innsbruck? Show me the view on this side."

Oberhauser bobbed into the hut and out again. The major fell in just behind him as he talked, point-

ing out this or that distant church spire or mountain peak.

They came to the point above the glacier. Major Smythe drew his revolver, and at a range of two feet, fired two bullets into the base of Hannes Oberhauser's skull. No muffing! Dead-on!

The impact of the bullets knocked the guide clean off his feet and over the edge. Major Smythe craned over. The body hit twice only, and then crashed onto the glacier. But not onto its fissured origin. Halfway down and on a patch of old snow! "Hell!" said Major Smythe.

The deep boom of the two shots, which had been batting to and fro among the mountains, died away. Major Smythe took one last look at the black splash on the white snow and hurried off along the shoulder. First things first!

He started on the top of the cairn, working as if the devil were after him, throwing the rough, heavy stones indiscriminately down the mountain to right or left. His hands began to bleed, but he hardly noticed. Now there were only two feet or so left, and nothing! Bloody nothing! He bent to the last pile, scrabbling feverishly. And then! Yes! The edge of a metal box. A few more rocks away, and there was the whole of it! A good old gray Wehrmacht ammunition box with the trace of some lettering still on it. Major Smythe gave a groan of joy. He sat down on a hard piece of rock, and his mind went orbiting through Bentleys, Monte Carlo, penthouse flats, Cartier's, champagne, caviar, and, incongruously (but because he loved golf), a new set of Henry Cotton irons.

Drunk with his dreams, Major Smythe sat there

looking at the gray box for a full quarter of an hour. Then he looked at his watch and got briskly to his feet. Time to get rid of the evidence. The box had a handle at each end. Major Smythe had expected it to be heavy. He had mentally compared its probable weight with the heaviest thing he had ever carried—a forty-pound salmon he had caught in Scotland just before the war—but the box was certainly double that weight, and he was only just able to lift it out of its last bed of rocks onto the thin alpine grass. Then he slung his handkerchief through one of the handles and dragged it clumsily along the shoulder to the hut. Then he sat down on the stone doorstep, and, his eyes never leaving the box, he tore at Oberhauser's smoked sausage with his strong teeth and thought about getting his fifty thousand pounds—for that was the figure he put it at—down the mountain and into a new hiding place.

Oberhauser's sausage was a real mountaineer's meal ——tough, well-fatted, and strongly garlicked. Bits of it stuck uncomfortably between Major Smythe's teeth. He dug them out with a sliver of matchstick and spat them on the ground. Then his Intelligence-wise mind came into operation, and he meticulously searched among the stones and grass, picked up the scraps, and swallowed them. From now on he was a criminal—as much a criminal as if he had robbed a bank and shot the guard. He was a cop turned robber. He *must* remember that! It would be death if he didn't —death instead of Cartier's. All he had to do was to take infinite pains. He would take those pains, and by God they would be infinite! Then, for ever after, he would be rich and happy. After taking ridiculously minute trouble to eradicate any sign of entry into the hut, he dragged the ammunition box to the edge of the last rock face and aiming it away from the glacier, tipped it, with a prayer, into space.

The gray box, turning slowly in the air, hit the first steep slope below the rock face, bounded another hundred feet, and landed with an iron clang in some loose scree and stopped. Major Smythe couldn't see if it had burst open. He didn't mind one way or the other. He had tried to open it without success. Let the mountain do it for him!

With a last look around, he went over the edge. He took great care at each piton, tested each handhold and foothold before he put his weight on it. Coming down, he was a much more valuable life than he had been climbing up. He made for the glacier and trudged across the melting snow to the black patch on the icefield. There was nothing to be done about footprints. It would take only a few days for them to be melted down by the sun. He got to the body. He had seen many corpses during the war, and the blood and broken limbs meant nothing to him. He dragged the remains of Oberhauser to the nearest deep crevasse and toppled it in. Then he went carefully around the lip of the crevasse and kicked the snow overhang down on top of the body. Then, satisfied with his work, he retraced his steps, placing his feet exactly in his old footprints, and made his way on down the slope to the ammunition box.

Yes, the mountain had burst open the lid for him. Almost casually he tore away the cartridge-paper wrappings. The two great hunks of metal glittered up at him under the sun. There were the same mark-

ings on each—the swastika in a circle below an eagle,
and the date 1943—the mint marks of the Reichsbank. Major Smythe gave a nod of approval. He replaced the paper and hammered the crooked lid half-
shut with a rock. Then he tied the lanyard of his
Webley around one of the handles and moved on
down the mountain, dragging his clumsy burden behind him.

It was now one o'clock, and the sun beat fiercely
down on his naked chest, frying him in his own sweat.
His reddened shoulders began to burn. So did his face.
To hell with them! He stopped at the stream from the
glacier, dipped his handkerchief in the water, and tied
it across his forehead. Then he drank deeply and went
on, occasionally cursing the ammunition box as it
caught up with him and banged at his heels. But these
discomforts, the sunburn and the bruises, were nothing
compared with what he would have to face when he
got down to the valley and the going leveled out. For
the time being he had gravity on his side. There would
come at least a mile when he would have to carry the
blasted stuff. Major Smythe winced at the thought of
the havoc the eighty pounds or so would wreak on
his burned back. "Oh well," he said to himself almost
lightheadedly, *"il faut souffrir pour être millionaire!"*

When he got to the bottom and the time had come,
he sat and rested on a mossy bank under the firs. Then
he spread out his bush shirt and and heaved the two
bars out of the box and onto its center and tied the
tails of the shirt as firmly as he could to where the
sleeves sprang from the shoulders. After digging a
shallow hole in the bank and burying the empty box,
he knotted the two cuffs of the sleeves firmly together,

knelt down and slipped his head through the rough
sling, got his hands on either side of the knot to
protect his neck, and staggered to his feet, crouching
far forward so as not to be pulled over on his back.
Then, crushed under half his own weight, his back on
fire under the contact with his burden, and his breath
rasping through his constricted lungs, coolie-like, he
shuffled slowly off down the little path through the
trees.

To this day he didn't know how he had made it to
the jeep. Again and again the knots gave under the
strain and the bars crashed down on the calves of his
legs, and each time he had sat with his head in his
hands and then started all over again. But finally, by
concentrating on counting his steps and stopping for
a rest at every hundredth, he got to the blessed little
jeep and collapsed beside it. And then there had been
the business of burying his hoard in the wood, amongst
a jumble of big rocks that he would be sure to find
again, of cleaning himself up as best he could, and of
getting back to his billet by a circuitous route that
avoided the Oberhauser chalet. And then it was all
done, and he had got drunk by himself off a bottle of
cheap schnapps and eaten and gone to bed and fallen
into a stupefied sleep. The next day, MOB "A" Force
had moved off up the Mittersill valley on a fresh trail,
and six months later Major Smythe was back in London and his war was over.

But not his problems. Gold is difficult stuff to
smuggle, certainly in the quantity available to Major
Smythe, and it was now essential to get his two bars
across the Channel and into a new hiding place. So
he put off his demobilization and clung to the red

tabs of his temporary rank, and particularly to his Military Intelligence passes, and soon got himself sent back to Germany as a British representative at the Combined Interrogation Center in Munich. There he did a scratch job for six months, during which, on a weekend's leave, he collected his gold and stowed it away in a battered suitcase in his quarters. Then he resigned his post and flew back to England, carrying the two bars in a bulky briefcase. The hundred yards across the tarmac at each end of the flight, and the handling of his case as if it contained only papers, required two benzedrine tablets and a will of iron, but at last he had his fortune safe in the basement of an aunt's flat in Kensington and could get on with the next phase of his plans at leisure.

He resigned from the Royal Marines and got himself demobilized and married one of the many girls he had slept with at MOB Force Headquarters, a charming blonde Wren from a solid middle-class family named Mary Parnell. He got passages for them both in one of the early banana boats sailing from Avonmouth to Kingston, Jamaica, which they both agreed would be a paradise of sunshine, good food, cheap drink, and a glorious haven from the gloom and restrictions and Labour Government of postwar England. Before they sailed, Major Smythe showed Mary the gold bars from which he had chiseled away the mint marks of the Reichsbank.

"I've been clever, darling," he said. "I just don't trust the pound these days, so I've sold out all my securities and swapped the lot for gold. Must be about fifty thousand pounds' worth there. That should

give us twenty-five years of the good life, just cutting off a slice now and then and selling it."

Mary Parnell was not to know that such a transaction was impossible under the currency laws. She knelt down and ran her hands lovingly over the gleaming bars. Then she got up and threw her arms around Major Smythe's neck and kissed him. "You're a wonderful, wonderful man," she said, almost in tears. "Frightfully clever and handsome and brave, and now I find out that you're rich as well. I'm the luckiest girl in the world."

"Well, anyway we're rich," said Major Smythe. "But promise me you won't breathe a word, or we'll have all the burglars in Jamaica around our ears. Promise?"

"Cross my heart."

Prince's Club, in the foothills above Kingston, was indeed a paradise. Pleasant enough members, wonderful servants, unlimited food, cheap drink—and all in the wonderful setting of the tropics, which neither of them had known before. They were a popular couple, and Major Smythe's war record earned them the entrée to Government House society, after which their life was one endless round of parties, with tennis for Mary and golf (with the Henry Cotton irons!) for Major Smythe. In the evenings there was bridge for her and the high poker game for him. Yes, it was paradise all right, while in their homeland people munched their Spam, fiddled in the black market, cursed the government, and suffered the worst winter's weather for thirty years.

The Smythes met all their initial expenditures from their combined cash reserves, swollen by wartime gratuities, and it took Major Smythe a full year of careful sniffing around before he decided to do business with the Messrs. Foo, import and export merchants. The brothers Foo, highly respected and very rich, were the acknowledged governing junta of the flourishing Chinese community in Jamaica. Some of their trading was suspected to be devious—in the Chinese tradition—but all Major Smythe's casually meticulous inquiries confirmed that they were utterly trustworthy. The Bretton Woods Convention, fixing a controlled world price for gold, had been signed, and it had already become common knowledge that Tangier and Macao were two free ports that, for different reasons, had escaped the Bretton Woods net; there a price of at least one hundred dollars per ounce of gold, ninety-nine fine, could be obtained, compared with the fixed world price of thirty-five dollars per ounce. And, conveniently, the Foos had just begun to trade again with a resurgent Hong Kong, already the port of entry for gold smuggling into the neighboring Macao. The whole setup was, in Major Smythe's language, "ticketty-boo." He had a most pleasant meeting with the Foo brothers. No questions were asked until it came to examining the bars. At this point the absence of mint marks resulted in a polite inquiry as to the original provenance of the gold.

"You see, Major," said the older and blander of the brothers behind the big bare mahogany desk, "in the bullion market the mint marks of all respectable national banks and responsible dealers are accepted without question. Such marks guarantee the fineness of the gold. But of course there are other banks and dealers whose methods of refining"—his benign smile widened a fraction—"are perhaps not quite, shall we say, so accurate."

"You mean the old gold brick swindle?" asked Major Smythe with a twinge of anxiety. "Hunk of lead covered with gold plating?"

Both brothers tee-heed reassuringly. "No, no, Major. That of course is out of the question. But"—the smiles held constant—"if you cannot recall the provenance of these fine bars, perhaps you would have no objections if we were to undertake an assay. There are methods of determining the exact fineness of such bars. My brother and I are competent in these methods. If you would care to leave these with us and perhaps come back after lunch . . . ?"

There had been no alternative. Major Smythe had to trust the Foos utterly now. They could cook up any figure, and he would just have to accept it. He went over to the Myrtle Bank and had one or two stiff drinks and a sandwich that stuck in his throat. Then he went back to the cool office of the Foos.

The setting was the same—the two smiling brothers, the two bars of gold, the briefcase—but now there was a piece of paper and a gold Parker pen in front of the older brother.

"We have solved the problem of your fine bars, Major——"

Fine! Thank God," thought Major Smythe.

"——And I am sure you will be interested to know their probable history."

"Yes indeed," said Major Smythe, with a brave show of enthusiasm.

"They are German bars, Major. Probably from the wartime Reichsbank. This we have deduced from the fact that they contain ten percent of lead. Under the Hitler regime, it was the foolish habit of the Reichsbank to adulterate their gold in this manner. This fact rapidly became known to dealers, and the price of German bars, in Switzerland for instance, where many of them found their way, was adjusted downward accordingly. So the only result of the German foolishness was that the national bank of Germany lost a reputation for honest dealing it had earned over the centuries." The Oriental's smile didn't vary. "Very bad business, Major. Very stupid."

Major Smythe marveled at the omniscience of these two men so far from the great commercial channels of the world, but he also cursed it. *Now what?* He said, "That's very interesting, Mr. Foo. But it is not very good news for me. Are these bars not 'Good delivery,' or whatever you call it in the bullion world?"

The older Foo made a slight throwaway gesture with his right hand. "It is of no importance, Major. Or rather, it is of very small importance. We will sell your gold at its true mint value, let us say, eighty-nine fine. It may be re-fined by the ultimate purchaser, or it may not. That is not our business. We shall have sold a true bill of goods."

"But at a lower price."

"That is so, Major. But I think I have some good news for you. Have you any estimate as to the worth of these two bars?"

"I thought around fifty thousand pounds."

The older Foo gave a dry chuckle. "I think—if we sell wisely and slowly—you should receive one hundred thousand pounds, Major, subject that is, to our commission, which will include shipping and incidental charges."

"How much would that be?"

"We were thinking about a figure of ten percent, Major. If that is satisfactory to you."

Major Smythe had an idea that bullion brokers received a fraction of one percent. But what the hell? He had already as good as made forty thousand pounds since lunch. He said "Done" and got up and reached his hand across the desk.

From then on, every quarter, he would visit the office of the Foos carrying an empty suitcase. On the broad desk there would be one thousand new Jamaican pounds in neat bundles and the two gold bars, which diminished inch by inch, together with a typed slip showing the amount sold and the price obtained in Macao. It was all very simple and friendly and highly businesslike, and Major Smythe didn't think that he was being submitted to any form of squeeze other than the duly recorded ten percent. In any case, he didn't particularly care. Four thousand net a year was good enough for him, and his only worry was that the income tax people would get after him and ask him what he was living on. He mentioned this possibility to the Foos. But they said he was not to worry, and for the next four quarters, there was only nine hundred pounds instead of a thousand on the table and no comment was made by either side. Squeeze had been administered in the right quarter.

And so the lazy, sunshiny days passed by for fifteen happy years. The Smythes both put on weight, and Major Smythe had the first of his two coronaries and was told by his doctor to cut down on his alcohol and cigarettes, to take life more easily, to avoid fats and fried food. Mary Smythe tried to be firm with him, but when he took to secret drinking and to a life of petty lies and evasions, she tried to backpedal on her attempts to control his self-indulgence. But she was too late. She had already become the symbol of the caretaker to Major Smythe, and he took to avoiding her. She berated him with not loving her anymore. And when the continual bickering became too much for her simple nature, she became a sleeping pill addict. And one night, after one flaming drunken row, she took an overdose—"just to show him." It was too much of an overdose and it killed her. The suicide was hushed up, but the cloud did Major Smythe no good socially, and he retreated to the North Shore, which, although only some thirty miles across the island from the capital, is, even in the small society of Jamaica, a different world. And there he had settled in Wavelets and, after his second coronary, was in the process of drinking himself to death when this man named Bond arrived on the scene with an alternative death warrant in his pocket.

Major Smythe looked at his watch. It was a few minutes after twelve o'clock. He got up and poured himself another stiff brandy and ginger ale and went out onto the lawn. James Bond was sitting under the sea almonds gazing out to sea. He didn't look up when Major Smythe pulled up another aluminum garden chair and put his drink on the grass beside him.

When Major Smythe had finished telling his story,

Bond said unemotionally, "Yes, that's more or less the way I figured it."

"Want me to write it all out and sign it?"

"You can if you like. But not for me. That'll be for the court-martial. Your old corps will be handling all that. I've got nothing to do with the legal aspects. I shall put in a report to my own Service of what you've told me, and they'll pass it on to the Royal Marines. Then I suppose it'll go to the Public Prosecutor via Scotland Yard."

"Could I ask a question?"

"Of course."

"How did they find out?"

"It was a small glacier. Oberhauser's body came out at the bottom of it earlier this year. When the spring snows melted. Some climbers found it. All his papers and everything were intact. His family identified him. Then it was just a question of working back. The bullets clinched it."

"But how did you get mixed up in the whole thing?"

"MOB Force was a responsibility of my, er, Service. The papers found their way to us. I happened to see the file. I had some spare time on my hands. I asked to be given the job of chasing up the man who did it."

"Why?"

James Bond looked Major Smythe squarely in the eyes. "It just happened that Oberhauser was a friend of mine. He taught me to ski before the war, when I was in my teens. He was a wonderful man. He was something of a father to me at a time when I happened to need one."

"Oh, I see." Major Smythe looked away. "I'm sorry."

James Bond got to his feet. "Well, I'll be getting back to Kingston." He held up a hand. "No, don't bother. I'll find my way to the car." He looked down at the older man. He said abruptly, almost harshly—perhaps, Major Smythe thought, to hide his embarrassment—"It'll be about a week before they send someone out to bring you home." Then he walked off across the lawn and through the house, and Major Smythe heard the iron whirr of the self-starter and the clatter of the gravel on the unkempt drive.

Major Smythe, questing for his prey along the reef, wondered what exactly those last words of the Bond man had meant. Inside the Pirelli his lips drew mirthlessly back from the stained teeth. It was obvious, really. It was just a version of the corny old act of leaving the guilty officer alone with his revolver. If the Bond man had wanted to, he could have telephoned Government House and had an officer of the Jamaica Regiment sent over to take Major Smythe into custody. Decent of him, in a way. Or was it? A suicide would be tidier, save a lot of paperwork and taxpayers' money.

Should he oblige the Bond man and be tidy? Join Mary in whatever place suicides go to? Or go through with it—the indignity, the dreary formalities, the headlines, the boredom and drabness of a life sentence that would inevitably end with his third coronary? Or should he defend himself—plead wartime, a struggle with Oberhauser, prisoner trying to escape, Oberhauser knowing of the gold cache, the natural temptation of Smythe to make away with the bullion, he, a poor officer of the commandos confronted with sudden wealth?

Should he dramatically throw himself on the mercy of the court? Suddenly Major Smythe saw himself in the dock—a splendid, upright figure, in the fine be-medaled blue and scarlet of the ceremonial uniform that was the traditional rig for courtmartial. (Had the moths got into the japanned box in the spare room at Wavelets? Had the damp? Luna would have to look to it.) A day in the sunshine, if the weather held. A good brushing. With the help of his corset, he could surely still get his forty-inch waist into the thirty-four-inch trousers Gieves had made for him twenty, thirty, years ago. And, down on the floor of the court, at Chatham probably, the Prisoners' Friend, some staunch fellow, at least of colonel's rank in deference to his own seniority, would be pleading his cause. And there was always the possibility of appeal to a higher court. Why, the whole affair might become a cause célèbre . . . he would sell his story to the papers, write a book. . . .

Major Smythe felt the excitement mounting in him. Careful, old boy! Careful! Remember what the good old snip-cock had said! He put his feet to the ground and had a rest amidst the dancing waves of the northeast trades that kept the North Shore so delightfully cool until the torrid months—August, September, October—of the hurricane season. He would soon be having his two pink gins, skimpy lunch, and happily sodden siesta, after which he would have to give all this more careful thought. And then there were cocktails with the Arundels and dinner at the Shaw Park

Beach Club with the Marchesis. Then some high bridge and home to his Seconal sleep. Cheered by the prospect of the familiar routine, the black shadow of Bond retreated into the background. Now then, scorp, where are you? Octopussy's waiting for her lunch! Major Smythe put his head down, and his mind freshly focused and his eyes questing, continued his leisurely swim along the shallow valley between the coral clumps that led out toward the white-fringed reef.

Almost at once he saw the two spiny antennae of a lobster, or rather of its cousin, the West Indian langouste, weaving inquisitively toward him, toward the turbulence he was creating, from a deep fissure under a coral boulder. From the thickness of the antennae, it would be a big one, three or four pounds! Normally, Major Smythe would have put his feet down and delicately stirred up the sand in front of the lair to bring the lobster farther out, for they are an inquisitive family. Then he would have speared it through the head and taken it back for lunch. But today there was only one prey in his mind, one shape to concentrate on—the shaggy, irregular silhouette of a scorpionfish. And, ten minutes later, he saw a clump of seaweedy rock on the white sand that wasn't just a clump of seaweedy rock. He put his feet softly down and watched the poison spines erect themselves along the back of the thing. It was a good-sized one, perhaps three-quarters of a pound. He got his three-pronged spear ready and inched forward. Now the red angry eyes of the fish were wide open and watching him. He would have to make a single quick lunge from as nearly the vertical as possible; otherwise, he knew from experience, the barbed prongs, needle-sharp though they were, would almost certainly bounce off the horny head of the beast. He swung his feet up off the ground and paddled forward very slowly, using his free hand as a fin. Now! He lunged forward and downward. But the scorpionfish had felt the tiny approaching shockwave of the spear. There was a flurry of sand, and it had shot up in a vertical takeoff and whirred, in almost birdlike flight, under Major Smythe's belly.

Major Smythe cursed and twisted around in the water. Yes, it had done what the scorpionfish so often does—gone for refuge to the nearest algae-covered rock, and there, confident in its superb camouflage, gone to ground on the seaweed. Major Smythe had only to swim a few feet, lunge down again, this time more accurately, and he had it, flapping and squirming on the end of his spear.

The excitement and the small exertion had caused Major Smythe to pant, and he felt the old pain across his chest lurking, ready to come at him. He put his feet down, and after driving his spear all the way through the fish, held it, still flapping desperately, out of the water. Then he slowly made his way back across the lagoon on foot and walked up the sand of his beach to the wooden bench under the sea-grape. Then he dropped the spear with its jerking quarry on the sand beside him and sat down to rest.

It was perhaps five minutes later that Major Smythe felt a curious numbness more or less in the region of his solar plexus. He looked casually down, and his whole body stiffened with horror and disbelief. A patch of his skin, about the size of a cricket ball, had turned white under his tan, and, in the center of the

patch, there were three punctures, one below the other,
topped by little beads of blood. Automatically, Major
Smythe wiped away the blood. The holes were only
the size of pinpricks. Major Smythe remembered the
rising flight of the scorpionfish, and he said aloud, with
awe in his voice, but without animosity, "You got
me, you bastard! By God, you got me!"

He sat very still, looking down at his body and remembering what it said about scorpionfish stings in
the book he had borrowed from the Institute and had
never returned—*Dangerous Marine Animals,* an
American publication. He delicately touched and then
prodded the white area around the punctures. Yes,
the skin had gone totally numb, and now a pulse of
pain began to throb beneath it. Very soon this would
become a shooting pain. Then the pain would begin
to lance all over his body and become so intense that
he would throw himself on the sand, screaming and
thrashing about, to rid himself of it. He would vomit
and foam at the mouth, and then delirium and con-
vulsions would take over until he lost consciousness.
Then, inevitably in his case, there would ensue cardiac
failure and death. According to the book the whole
cycle would be complete in about a quarter of an hour
—that was all he had left—fifteen minutes of hideous
agony! There were cures, of course—procaine, anti-
biotics and antihistamines—if his weak heart would
stand them. But they had to be near at hand. Even
if he could climb the steps up to the house, and sup-
posing Dr. Cahusac had these modern drugs, the doctor couldn't possibly get to Wavelets in under an hour.

The first jet of pain seared into Major Smythe's
body and bent him over double. Then came another

and another, radiating through his stomach and limbs. Now there was a dry, metallic taste in his mouth, and his lips were prickling. He gave a groan and toppled off the seat onto the beach. A flapping on the sand beside his head reminded him of the scorpionfish. There came a lull in the spasms of pain. Instead, his whole body felt as though it was on fire, but, beneath the agony, his brain cleared. But of course! The experiment! Somehow, somehow he must get out to Octopussy and give her her lunch!

"Oh Pussy, my Pussy, this is the last meal you'll get."

Major Smythe mouthed the refrain to himself as he crouched on all fours, found his mask, and struggled to force it over his face. Then he got hold of his spear, tipped with the still flapping fish, and clutching his stomach with his free hand, crawled and slithered down the sand and into the water.

It was fifty yards of shallow water to the lair of the octopus in the coral cranny, and Major Smythe, screaming all the while into his mask, crawling mostly on his knees, somehow made it. As he came to the last approach and the water became deeper, he had to get to his feet, and the pain made him jiggle to and fro, as if he were a puppet manipulated by strings. Then he was there, and with a supreme effort of will, he held himself steady as he dipped his head down to let some water into his mask and clear the mist of his screams from the glass. Then, blood pouring from his bitten lower lip, he bent carefully down to look into Octopussy's house. Yes! The brown mass was still there. It was stirring excitedly. Why? Major Smythe saw the dark strings of his blood curling lazily down through the water. Of course! The darling was tasting his blood. A shaft of pain hit Major Smythe and sent him reeling. He heard himself babbling deliriously into his mask. *Pull yourself together, Dexter, old boy! You've got to give Pussy her lunch!* He steadied himself, and holding the spear well down the shaft, lowered the fish down toward the writhing hole.

Would Pussy take the bait? The poisonous bait that was killing Major Smythe but to which an octopus might be immune? If only Bengry could be here to watch! Three tentacles, weaving excitedly, came out of the hole and wavered around the scorpionfish. Now there was a gray mist in front of Major Smythe's eyes. He recognized it as the edge of unconsciousness and feebly shook his head to clear it. And then the tentacles leaped! But not at the fish! At Major Smythe's hand and arm. Major Smythe's torn mouth stretched in a grimace of pleasure. Now he and Pussy had shaken hands! How exciting! How truly wonderful!

But then the octopus, quietly, relentlessly pulled downward, and terrible realization came to Major Smythe. He summoned his dregs of strength and plunged his spear down. The only effect was to push the scorpionfish into the mass of the octopus and offer more arm to the octopus. The tentacles snaked upward and pulled more relentlessly. Too late, Major Smythe scrabbled away his mask. One bottled scream burst out across the empty bay, then his head went under and down, and there was an explosion of bubbles to the surface. Then Major Smythe's legs came up and the small waves washed his body to and fro while the octopus explored his right hand with its buccal orifice and took a first tentative bite at a finger with its beaklike jaws.

The body was found by two young Jamaicans spinning for needlefish from a canoe. They speared the octopus with Major Smythe's spear, killed it in the traditional fashion by turning it inside out and biting its head off, and brought the three corpses home. They turned Major Smythe's body over to the police, and had the scorpionfish and the seacat for supper.

The local correspondent of the *Daily Gleaner* reported that Major Smythe had been killed by an octopus, but the paper translated this into "found drowned" so as not to frighten away the tourists.

Later, in London, James Bond, privately assuming "suicide," wrote the same verdict of "found drowned," together with the date, on the last page and closed the bulky file.

It is only from the notes of Dr. Cahusac, who performed the autopsy, that it has been possible to construct some kind of a postscript to the bizarre and pathetic end of a once valuable officer of the Secret Service.

Lager or the heavy Beres... these days. But I can now?

THE LIVING DAYLIGHTS

J ames Bond lay in the five-hundred-yard firing point of the famous Century Range at Bisley. The white peg in the grass beside him said 44, and the same number was repeated high up on the distant butt above the single six-feet-square target that, to the human eye and in the late summer dusk, looked no larger than a postage stamp. But through Bond's glass—an infrared sniperscope fixed above his rifle—the lens covered the whole canvas. He could even clearly distinguish the pale blue and beige colors in which the target was divided, and the six-inch semicircular bull's-eye looked as big as the half-moon that was already beginning to show low down in the darkening sky above the distant crest of Chobham Ridges.

James Bond's last shot had been an inner left. Not good enough. He took another glance at the yellow and blue wind flags. They were streaming across range from the east rather more stiffly than when he had begun his shoot half an hour before, and he set two clicks more to the right on the wind gauge and traversed the cross-wires on the sniperscope back to the point of aim. Then he settled himself, put his trigger finger gently inside the guard and onto the curve of the trigger, shallowed his breathing, and very, very softly squeezed.

The vicious crack of the shot boomed across the empty range. The target disappeared below ground, and at once the dummy came up in its place. Yes. The black panel was in the bottom right-hand corner this time, not in the bottom left. A bull's-eye.

"Good," said the voice of the chief range officer from behind and above him. "Stay with it."

The target was already up again, and Bond put his cheek back to its warm patch on the chunky wooden stock and his eye to the rubber eyepiece of the scope. He wiped his gun hand down the side of his trousers and took the pistol grip that jutted sharply down below the trigger guard. He splayed his legs an inch more. Now there were to be five rounds rapid. It would be interesting to see if that would produce "fade." He guessed not. This extraordinary weapon the armorer had somehow got his hands on gave one the feeling that a standing man at a mile would be easy meat. It was mostly a .308-caliber International Experimental Target rifle built by Winchester to help American marksmen at World Championships, and it had the usual gadgets of superaccurate target weapons —a curled aluminum hand at the back of the butt that extended under the armpit and held the stock firmly into the shoulder, and an adjustable pinion

below the rifle's center of gravity to allow the stock to
be nailed into its grooved wooden rest. The armorer
had had the usual single-shot bolt action replaced by
a five-shot magazine, and he had assured Bond that if
he allowed as little as two seconds between shots to
steady the weapon there would be no fade even at
five hundred yards. For the job that Bond had to do,
he guessed that two seconds might be a dangerous loss
of time if he missed with his first shot. Anyway, M.
had said that the range would be not more than three
hundred yards. Bond would cut it down to one second
—almost continuous fire.

"Ready?"

"Yes."

"I'll give you a countdown from five. Now! Five,
four, three, two, one. Fire!"

The ground shuddered slightly and the air sang as
the five whirling scraps of cupronickel spat off into
the dusk. The target went down and quickly rose again,
decorated with four small white discs closely grouped
on the bull's-eye. There was no fifth disc—not even a
black one to show an inner or an outer.

"The last round was low," said the range officer
lowering his nightglasses. "Thanks for the contribu-
tion. We sift the sand on those butts at the end of
every year. Never get less than fifteen tons of good
lead and copper scrap out of them. Good money."

Bond had got to his feet. Corporal Menzies from
the armorers' section appeared from the pavilion of
the Gun Club and knelt down to dismantle the Winchester and its rest. He looked up at Bond. He said
with a hint of criticism, "You were taking it a bit fast,
sir. Last round was bound to jump wide."

"I know, corporal. I wanted to see how fast I *could* take it. I'm not blaming the weapon. It's a hell of a fine job. Please tell the armorer so from me. Now I'd better get moving. You're finding your own way back to London, aren't you?"

"Yes. Good night, sir."

The chief range officer handed Bond a record of his shoot—two sighting shots and then ten rounds at each hundred yards up to five hundred. "Damned good firing with this visibility. You ought to come back next year and have a bash at the Queen's Prize. It's open to all comers nowadays—British Commonwealth, that is."

"Thanks. Trouble is, I'm not all that much in England. And thanks for spotting for me." Bond glanced at the distant clock tower. On either side, the red danger flag and the red signal drum were coming down to show that firing had ceased. The hands stood at nine-fifteen. "I'd like to buy you a drink, but I've got an appointment in London. Can we hold it over until that Queen's Prize you were talking about?"

The range officer nodded noncommittally. He had been looking forward to finding out more about this man who had appeared out of the blue after a flurry of signals from the Ministry of Defense and had then proceeded to score well over ninety percent at all distances. And that after the range was closed for the night and visibility was poor-to-bad. And why had he, who only officiated at the annual July meeting, been ordered to be present? And why had he been told to see that Bond had a six-inch bull's-eye at five hundred instead of the regulation fifteen-inch? And why this flummery with the danger flag and signal drum that were only used on ceremonial occasions? To put pressure on the man? To give an edge of urgency to the shoot? Bond. Commander James Bond. The N.R.A. would surely have a record of anyone who could shoot like that. He'd remember to give them a call. Funny time to have an appointment in London. Probably a girl. The range officer's undistinguished face assumed a disgruntled expression. Sort of fellow who got all the girls he wanted.

The two men walked through the handsome façade of Club Row behind the range to Bond's car, which stood opposite the bullet-pitted iron reproduction of Landseer's famous Running Deer.

"Nice-looking job," commented the range officer. "Never seen a body like that on a Continental. Have it made specially?"

"Yes. The Mark IV's are anyway really only two-seaters. And damned little luggage space. So I got Mulliner's to make it into a real two-seater with plenty of trunk space. Selfish car I'm afraid. Well, good night. And thanks again." The twin exhausts boomed healthily, and the back wheels briefly spat gravel.

The chief range officer watched the ruby lights vanish up King's Avenue toward the London Road. He turned on his heel and went to find Corporal Menzies on a search for information that was to prove fruitless. The corporal remained as wooden as the big mahogany box he was in the process of loading into a khaki Land Rover without military symbols. The range officer was a major. He tried pulling his rank without success. The Land Rover hammered away in Bond's wake. The major walked moodily off to the offices of the National Rifle Association to try and find out what he wanted in the library under "Bond, J."

James Bond's appointment was not with a girl. It was with a B.E.A. flight to Hanover and Berlin. As he bit off the miles to London Airport, pushing the big car hard so as to have plenty of time for a drink, three drinks, before the takeoff, only part of his mind was on the road. The rest was reexamining, for the umpteenth time, the sequence that was now leading him to an appointment with an airplane. But only an interim appointment. His final rendezvous on one of the next three nights in Berlin was with a man. He had to see this man and he had to be sure to shoot him dead.

When, at around two-thirty that afternoon, James Bond had gone in through the double padded doors and had sat down opposite the turned-away profile on the other side of the big desk, he had sensed trouble. There was no greeting. M.'s head was sunk into his stiff turned-down collar in a Churchillian pose of gloomy reflection, and there was a droop of bitterness at the corner of his lips. He swiveled his chair around to face Bond, gave him an appraising glance as if, Bond thought, to see that his tie was straight and his hair properly brushed, and then began speaking, fast, biting off his sentences as if he wanted to be rid of what he was saying, and of Bond, as quickly as possible.

"Number 272. He's a good man. You won't have come across him. Simple reason that he's been holed up in Novaya Zemlya since the war. Now he's trying to get out—loaded with stuff. Atomic and rockets.

And their plan for a whole new series of tests. For nineteen sixty-one. To put the heat on the West. Something to do with Berlin. Don't quite get the picture, but the FO says if it's true it's terrific. Makes nonsense of the Geneva Conference and all this blather about nuclear disarmament the Communist bloc is putting out. He's got as far as East Berlin. But he's got practically the whole of the KGB on his tail—and the East German security forces of course. He's holed up somewhere in East Berlin, and he got one message over to us. That he'd be coming across between six and seven P.M. on one of the next three nights— tomorrow, next day, or next day. He gave the crossing point. Trouble is"—the downward curve of M.'s lips became even more bitter—"the courier he used was a double. Station WB bowled him out yesterday. Quite by chance. Had a lucky break with one of the KGB codes. The courier'll be flown out for trial, of course. But that won't help. The KGB knows that 272 will be making a run for it. They know when. They know where. They know just as much as we do—and no more. Now, the code we cracked was a one-day-only setting on their machines. But we got the whole of that day's traffic, and that was good enough. They plan to shoot him on the run. At this street crossing between East and West Berlin he gave us in his message. They're mounting quite an operation—Operation Extase, they call it. Put their best sniper on the job. All we know about him is that his code name is the Russian for Trigger. Station WB guesses he's the same man they've used before for sniper work. Long-range stuff across the frontier. He's going to be guarding this crossing every night, and his job is to get

272. Of course they'd obviously prefer to do a smoother job with machine guns and what-have-you. But it's quiet in Berlin at the moment, and apparently the word is it's got to stay so. Anyway"—M. shrugged —"they've got confidence in this Trigger operator, and that's the way it's going to be!"

"Where do I come in, sir?" But James Bond had guessed the answer, guessed why M. was showing his dislike of the whole business. This was going to be dirty work, and Bond, because he belonged to the Double-O Section, had been chosen for it. Perversely, Bond wanted to force M. to put it in black and white. This was going to be bad news, dirty news; and he didn't want to hear it from one of the section officers, or even from the Chief of Staff. This was to be murder. All right. Let M. bloody well say so.

"Where do you come in, 007?" M. looked coldly across the desk. "You know where you come in. You've got to kill this sniper. And you've got to kill him before he gets 272. That's all. Is that understood?" The clear blue eyes remained cold as ice. But Bond knew that they remained so only with an effort of will. M. didn't like sending any man to a killing. But, when it had to be done, he always put on this fierce, cold act of command. Bond knew why. It was to take some of the pressure, some of the guilt, off the killer's shoulders.

So now Bond, who knew these things, decided to make it easy and quick for M. He got to his feet. "That's all right, sir. I suppose the Chief of Staff has got all the gen. I'd better go and put in some practice. It wouldn't do to miss." He walked to the door.

M. said quietly, "Sorry to have to hand this to you. Nasty job. But it's got to be done well."

"I'll do my best, sir." James Bond walked out and closed the door behind him. He didn't like the job, but on the whole he'd rather have it himself than have the responsibility of ordering someone else to go and do it.

The Chief of Staff had been only a shade more sympathetic. "Sorry you've bought this one, James," he had said. "But Tanqueray was definite that he hadn't got anyone good enough on his station, and this isn't the sort of job you can ask a regular soldier to do. Plenty of top marksmen in the B.A.O.R., but a live target needs another kind of nerve. Anyway, I've been on to Bisley and fixed a shoot for you to-night at eight-fifteen when the ranges will be closed. Visibility should be about the same as you'll be getting in Berlin around an hour earlier. The armorer's got the gun—a real target job—and he's sending it down with one of his men. You'll find your own way. Then you're booked on a midnight B.E.A. charter flight to Berlin. Take a taxi to this address." He handed Bond a piece of paper. "Go up to the fourth floor, and you'll find Tanqueray's Number Two waiting for you. Then I'm afraid you'll just have to sit it out for the next three days."

"How about the gun? Am I supposed to take it through the German customs in a golfbag or something?"

The Chief of Staff hadn't been amused. "It'll go over in the FO pouch. You'll have it by tomorrow midday." He had reached for a signal pad. "Well,

you'd better get cracking. I'll just let Tanqueray
know everything's fixed."

James Bond glanced down at the dim blue face of
the dashboard clock. Ten-fifteen. With any luck, by
this time tomorrow it would all be finished. After
all, it was the life of this man Trigger against the life
of 272. It wasn't *exactly* murder. Pretty near it,
though. He gave a vicious blast on his triple wind
horns at an inoffensive family saloon, took the round-
about in a quite unnecessary dry skid, wrenched the
wheel harshly to correct it, and pointed the nose of
the Bentley toward the distant glow that was London
Airport.

The ugly six-story building at the corner of the
Kochstrasse and the Wilhelmstrasse was the only one
standing in a waste of empty bombed space. Bond
paid off his taxi and got a brief impression of the
neighborhood—waist-high weeds and half-tidied rubble walls stretching away to a big deserted crossroads
lit by a central cluster of yellowish arc lamps—before
he pushed the bell for the fourth floor and at once
heard the click of the door opener. The door closed
itself behind him, and he walked over the uncarpeted
cement floor to the old-fashioned lift. The smell of
cabbage, cheap cigar smoke, and stale sweat reminded
him of other apartment houses in Germany and Central Europe. Even the sigh and faint squeal of the slow
lift were part of a hundred assignments when he had
been fired off by M., like a projectile, at some distant
target where a problem waited for his coming, waited
to be solved by him. At least this time the reception

committee was on his side. This time there was nothing
to fear at the top of the stairs.

Number Two of Secret Service Station WB was a
lean, tense man in his early forties. He wore the uniform of his profession—well-cut, well-used, light-
weight tweeds in a dark green herringbone, a soft
white silk shirt, and an old school tie (in his case
Wykehamist). At the sight of the tie, and while they
exchanged conventional greetings in the small musty
lobby of the apartment, Bond's spirits, already low,
sank another degree. He knew the type—backbone
of the civil service . . . overcrammed and underloved
at Winchester . . . a good second in P.P.E. at Oxford
. . . the war, staff jobs he would have done meticulously
—perhaps an O.B.E. . . . Allied Control Commission
in Germany where he had been recruited into the I
Branch. . . . And thence—because he was the ideal
staff man and A-one with Security, and because he
thought he would find life, drama, romance—the
things he had never had—into the Secret Service. A
sober, careful man had been needed to chaperone
Bond on this ugly business. Captain Paul Sender, late
of the Welsh Guards, had been the obvious choice.
He had bought it. Now, like a good Wykehamist, he
concealed his distaste for the job beneath careful, trite
conversation as he showed Bond the layout of the
apartment and the arrangements that had been made
for the executioner's preparedness and, to a modest
extent, his comfort.

The flat consisted of a large double bedroom, a
bathroom, and a kitchen containing tinned food, milk,
butter, eggs, bread, and one bottle of Dimple Haig.
The only odd feature in the bedroom was that one of

the double beds was angled up against the curtains covering the single broad window and was piled high with three mattresses below the bedclothes.

Captain Sender said, "Care to have a look at the field of fire? Then I can explain what the other side has in mind."

Bond was tired. He didn't particularly want to go to sleep with the picture of the battlefield on his mind. But he said, "That'd be fine."

Captain Sender switched off the lights. Chinks from the streetlight at the intersection showed round the curtains. "Don't want to draw the curtains," said Captain Sender. "Unlikely, but they may be on the lookout for a covering party for 272. If you'd just lie on the bed and get your head under the curtains, I'll brief you about what you'll be looking at. Look to the left."

It was a sash window, and the bottom half was open. The mattresses, by design, gave only a little, and James Bond found himself more or less in the firing position he had been in on the Century Range. But now he was staring across broken, thickly weeded bombed ground toward the bright river of the Zimmerstrasse—the border with East Berlin. It looked about a hundred and fifty yards away. Captain Sender's voice from above him and behind the curtain began reciting. It reminded Bond of a spiritualist séance.

"That's bombed ground in front of you. Plenty of cover. A hundred and thirty yards of it up to the frontier. Then the frontier—the street—and then a big stretch of more bombed ground on the enemy side. That's why 272 chose this route. It's one of the few places in the town which is broken land—thick weeds, ruined walls, cellars—on both sides of the frontier. . . . 272 will sneak through that mess on the other side, and make a dash across the Zimmerstrasse for the mess on our side. Trouble is, he'll have thirty yards of brightly lit frontier to sprint across. That'll be the killing ground. Right?"

Bond said, "Yes." He said it softly. The scent of the enemy, the need to take care, already had him by the nerves.

"To your left, that big new ten-story block is the Haus der Ministerien, the chief brain center of East Berlin. You can see the lights are still on in most of the windows. Most of those will stay on all night. These chaps work hard—shifts all round the clock. You probably won't need to worry about the lighted ones. This Trigger chap will almost certainly fire from one of the dark windows. You'll see there's a block of four together on the corner above the intersection. They've stayed dark last night and tonight. They've got the best field of fire. From here, their range varies from three hundred to three hundred and ten yards. I've got all the figures and so on when you want them. You needn't worry about much else. That street stays empty during the night—only the motorized patrols about every half an hour. Light armored car with a couple of motorcycles as escort. Last night, which I suppose is typical, between six and seven when this thing's going to be done, there were a few people that came and went out of that side door. Civil-servant types. Before that nothing out of the ordinary—usual flow of people in and out of a busy government building, except, of all things, a whole damned woman's orchestra. Made a hell of a racket in some concert hall they've got in there. Part of the block is the Ministry of Culture. Otherwise nothing—certainly none of the KGB people we know, or any signs of preparation for a job like this. But there wouldn't be. They're careful chaps, the opposition. Anyway, have a good look. Don't forget it's darker than it will be tomorrow around six. But you can get the general picture."

Bond got the general picture, and it stayed with him long after the other man was asleep and snoring softly with a gentle regular clicking sound. A Wykehamist snore, Bond reflected irritably.

Yes, he had got the picture. The picture of a flicker of movement among the shadowy ruins on the other side of the gleaming river of light, a pause, the wild zigzagging sprint of a man in the full glare of the arcs, the crash of gunfire—and then either a crumpled, sprawling heap in the middle of the wide street or the noise of his onward dash through the weeds and rubble of the Western Sector. Sudden death or a home run. The true gauntlet! How much time would Bond have to spot the Russian sniper in one of those dark windows? And kill him? Five seconds? Ten? When dawn edged the curtains with gun metal, Bond capitulated to his fretting mind. It had won. He went softly into the bathroom and surveyed the ranks of medicine bottles that a thoughtful Secret Service had provided to keep its executioner in good shape. He selected the Tuinal, chased down two of the ruby and blue depthcharges with a glass of water, and went back to bed. Then, poleaxed, he slept.

He awoke at midday. The flat was empty. Bond drew the curtains to let in the gray Prussian day, and, standing well back from the window, gazed out

at the drabness of Berlin, and listened to the tram
noises and to the distant screeching of the U-Bahn as
it took the big curve into the Zoo Station. He gave a
quick, reluctant glance at what he had examined the
night before, noted that the weeds among the bomb
rubble were much the same as the London ones—
campion, dock, and bracken—and then went into the
kitchen.

There was a note propped against a loaf of bread:
"My friend [a Secret Service euphemism that in this
context meant Sender's chief] says it's all right for
you to go out. But to be back by 1700 hours. Your
gear [doubletalk for Bond's rifle] has arrived and the
batman will lay it out this P.M. P. Sender."

Bond lit the gas cooker, and with a sneer at his
profession, burned the message. Then he brewed
himself a vast dish of scrambled eggs and bacon,
which he heaped on buttered toast and washed down
with black coffee into which he had poured a liberal
tot of whiskey. Then he bathed and shaved, dressed
in the drab, anonymous, middle-European clothes
he had brought over for the purpose, looked at his
disordered bed, decided to hell with it, and went
down in the lift and out of the building.

James Bond had always found Berlin a glum, inimical city, varnished on the Western side with a brittle
veneer of gimcrack polish rather like the chromium
trim on American motorcars. He walked to the Kur-
fürstendamm and sat in the Café Marquardt and drank
an espresso and moodily watched the obedient queues
of pedestrians waiting for the Go sign on the traffic
lights while the shiny stream of cars went through
their dangerous quadrille at the busy intersection.

It was cold outside and the sharp wind from the Russian steppes whipped at the girls' skirts and at the waterproofs of the impatient hurrying men, each with the inevitable briefcase tucked under his arm. The infrared wall heaters in the café glared redly down and gave a spurious glow to the faces of the café squatters, consuming their traditional "one cup of coffee and ten glasses of water," reading the free newspapers and periodicals in their wooden racks, earnestly bending over business documents. Bond, closing his mind to the evening, debated with himself about ways to spend the afternoon. It finally came down to a choice between a visit to that respectable-looking brownstone house in the Clausewitzstrasse known to all concierges and taxi drivers and a trip to the Wannsee and a strenuous walk in the Grunewald. Virtue triumphed. Bond paid for his coffee and went out into the cold and took a taxi to the Zoo Station.

The pretty young trees round the long lake had already been touched by the breath of autumn, and there was occasional gold amongst the green. Bond walked hard for two hours along the leafy paths, then chose a restaurant with a glassed-in veranda above the lake and greatly enjoyed a high tea consisting of a double portion of *Matjeshering,* smothered in cream and onion rings, and two *Molle mit Korn.* (This Berlin equivalent of a boilermaker and his assistant was a schnapps, double, washed down with draught Löwenbräu.) Then, feeling more encouraged, he took the S-Bahn back into the city.

Outside the apartment house, a nondescript young man was tinkering with the engine of a black Opel Kapitan. He didn't take his head out from under the bonnet when Bond passed close by him and went up to the door and pressed the bell.

Captain Sender was reassuring. It was a "friend" —a corporal from the transport section of Station WB. He had fixed up some bad engine trouble on the Opel. Each night, from six to seven, he would be ready to produce a series of multiple backfires when a signal on a walkie-talkie operated by Sender told him to do so. This would give some kind of cover for the noise of Bond's shooting. Otherwise, the neighborhood might alert the police and there would be a lot of untidy explaining to be done. Their hideout was in the American Sector, and while their American "friends" had given Station WB clearance for this operation, the "friends" were naturally anxious that it should be a clean job and without repercussions.

Bond was suitably impressed by the car gimmick, as he was by the very workmanlike preparations that had been made for him in the living room. Here, behind the head of his high bed, giving a perfect firing position, a wood and metal stand had been erected against the broad windowsill, and along it lay the Winchester, the tip of its barrel just denting the curtains. The wood and all the metal parts of the rifle and sniperscope had been painted a dull black, and, laid out on the bed like sinister evening clothes, was a black velvet hood stitched to a waist-length shirt of the same material. The hood had wide slits for the eyes and mouth. It reminded Bond of old prints of the Spanish Inquisition or of the anonymous operators on the guillotine platform during the French Revolution. There was a similar hood on Captain Sender's bed, and on his section of the windowsill there

lay a pair of nightglasses and the microphone for the walkie-talkie.

Captain Sender, his face worried and tense with nerves, said there was no news at the Station, no change in the situation as they knew it. Did Bond want anything to eat? Or a cup of tea? Perhaps a tranquilizer—there were several kinds in the bathroom?

Bond stitched a cheerful, relaxed expression on his face and said no thanks, and gave a lighthearted account of his day while an artery near his solar plexus began thumping gently as tension built up inside him like a watchspring tightening. Finally his small talk petered out and he lay down on his bed with a German thriller he had bought on his wanderings, while Captain Sender moved fretfully about the flat, looking too often at his watch and chainsmoking Kent filter-tips through (he was a careful man) a Dunhill filtered cigarette holder.

James Bond's choice of reading matter, prompted by a spectacular jacket of a half-naked girl strapped to a bed, turned out to have been a happy one for the occasion. It was called *Verderbt, Verdammt, Verraten*. The prefix *ver* signified that the girl had not only been ruined, damned, and betrayed, but that she had suffered these misfortunes most thoroughly. James Bond temporarily lost himself in the tribulations of the heroine, Gräfin Liselotte Mutzenbacher, and it was with irritation that he heard Captain Sender say that it was five-thirty and time to take up their positions.

Bond took off his coat and tie, put two sticks of chewing gum in his mouth, and donned the hood.

The lights were switched off by Captain Sender, and Bond lay along the bed, got his eye to the eyepiece of the sniperscope, and gently lifted the bottom edge of the curtain back and over his shoulders.

Now dusk was approaching, but otherwise the scene (a year later to become famous as Checkpoint Charlie) was like a well-remembered photograph— the wasteland in front of him, the bright river of the frontier road, the further wasteland, and, on the left, the ugly square block of the Haus der Ministerien with its lit and dark windows. Bond scanned it all slowly, moving the sniperscope, with the rifle, by means of the precision screws on the wooden base. It was all the same except that now there was a trickle of personnel leaving and entering the Haus der Ministerien through the door onto the Wilhelmstrasse. Bond looked long at the four dark windows—dark again tonight—that he agreed with Sender were the enemy's firing points. The curtains were drawn back, and the sash windows were wide open at the bottom. Bond's scope could not penetrate into the rooms, but there was no sign of movement within the four oblong black gaping mouths.

Now there was extra traffic in the street below the windows. The woman's orchestra came trooping down the pavement toward the entrance. Twenty laughing, talking girls carrying their instruments—violin and wind instrument cases, satchels with their scores—and four of them with the drums. A gay, happy little crocodile. Bond was reflecting that some people still seemed to find life fun in the Soviet Sector, when his glasses picked out and stayed on the girl carrying the cello. Bond's masticating jaws stopped still, and then reflectively went on with their chewing as he twisted the screw to depress the sniperscope and keep her in its center.

The girl was taller than the others, and her long, straight, fair hair, falling to her shoulders, shone like molten gold under the arcs at the intersection. She was hurrying along in a charming, excited way, carrying the cello case as if it were no heavier than a violin. Everything was flying—the skirt of her coat, her feet, her hair. She was vivid with movement and life and, it seemed, with gaiety and happiness as she chattered to the two girls who flanked her and laughed back at what she was saying. As she turned in at the entrance amidst her troupe, the arcs momentarily caught a beautiful, pale profile. And then she was gone, and, it seemed to Bond, that with her disappearance, a stab of grief lanced into his heart. How odd! How very odd! This had not happened to him since he was young. And now this single girl, seen only indistinctly and far away, had caused him to suffer this sharp pang of longing, this thrill of animal magnetism! Morosely, Bond glanced down at the luminous dial of his watch. Five-fifty. Only ten minutes to go. No transport arriving at the entrance. None of those anonymous black Zik saloons he had half-expected. He closed as much of his mind as he could to the girl and sharpened his wits. Get on, damn you! Get back to your job!

From somewhere inside the Haus der Ministerien there came the familiar sounds of an orchestra tuning up—the strings tuning their instruments to single notes on the piano, the sharp blare of individual woodwinds—then a pause, and then the collective crash of melody as the whole orchestra threw itself competently, so far as Bond could judge, into the opening bars of what even to James Bond was vaguely familiar.

"Moussorgsky's Overture to *Boris Godunov*," said Captain Sender succinctly. "Anyway, six o'clock coming up." And then, urgently, "Hey! Right-hand bottom of the four windows! Watch out!"

Bond depressed the sniperscope. Yes, there was movement inside the black cave. Now, from the interior, a thick black object, a weapon, had slid out. It moved firmly, minutely, swiveling down and sideways so as to cover the stretch of the Zimmerstrasse between the two wastelands of rubble. Then the unseen operator in the room behind seemed satisfied, and the weapon remained still, fixed obviously to such a stand as Bond had beneath his rifle.

"What is it? What sort of gun?" Captain Sender's voice was more breathless than it should have been.

Take it easy, dammit! thought Bond. It's me who's supposed to have the nerves.

He strained his eyes, taking in the squat flash eliminator at the muzzle, the telescopic sight, and the thick downward chunk of magazine. Yes, that would be it! Absolutely for sure—and the best they had!

"Kalashnikov," he said curtly. "Submachinegun. Gas-operated. Thirty rounds in seven sixty-two millimeter. Favorite with the KGB. They're going to do a saturation job after all. Perfect for range. We'll have to get him pretty quick, or 272 will end up not just dead but strawberry jam. You keep an eye out for any movement over there in the rubble. I'll have to stay married to that window and the gun. He'll have to show himself to fire. Other chaps are probably

spotting behind him—perhaps from all four windows.
Much the sort of setup we expected, but I didn't think
they'd use a weapon that's going to make all the racket
this one will. Should have known they would. A running man will be hard to get in this light with a single-
shot job."

Bond fiddled minutely with the traversing and
elevating screws at his fingertips and got the fine
lines of the scope exactly intersected, just behind where
the butt of the enemy gun merged into the blackness
behind. Get the chest—don't bother about the head!

Inside the hood, Bond's face began to sweat and
his eye socket was slippery against the rubber of the
eyepiece. That didn't matter. It was only his hands,
his trigger finger, that must stay bone dry. As the
minutes ticked by, he frequently blinked his eyes to
rest them, shifted his limbs to keep them supple, listened to the music to relax his mind.

The minutes slouched on leaden feet. How old
would she be? Early twenties? Say twenty-three? With
that poise and insouciance, the hint of authority in her
long easy stride, she would come of good racy stock—
one of the old Prussian families probably or from similar remnants in Poland or even Russia. Why in hell
did she have to choose the cello? There was something
almost indecent in the idea of this bulbous, ungainly
instrument between her splayed thighs. Of course Sug-
gia had managed to look elegant, and so did that girl
Amaryllis somebody. But they should invent a way
for women to play the damned thing sidesaddle.

From his side Captain Sender said, "Seven o'clock.
Nothing's stirred on the other side. Bit of movement
on our side, near a cellar close to the frontier. That'll

be our reception committee—two good men from the Station. Better stay with it until they close down. Let me know when they take that gun in."

"All right."

It was seven-thirty when the KGB submachinegun was gently drawn back into the black interior. One by one the bottom sashes of the four windows were closed. The coldhearted game was over for the night. 272 was still holed up. Two more nights to go!

Bond softly drew the curtain over his shoulders and across the muzzle of the Winchester. He got up, pulled off his cowl, and went into the bathroom, where he stripped and had a shower. Then he had two large whiskeys-on-the-rocks in quick succession, while he waited, his ears pricked, for the now muffled sound of the orchestra to stop. At eight o'clock it did, with the expert comment from Sender—"Borodin's *Prince Igor*, Choral Dance Number 17, I think."—who had been getting off his report in garbled language to the Head of Station.

"Just going to have another look. I've rather taken to that tall blonde with the cello," Bond said to Sender.

"Didn't notice her," said Sender, uninterested. He went into the kitchen. Tea, guessed Bond. Or perhaps Horlick's. Bond donned his cowl, went back to his firing position, and depressed the sniperscope to the doorway of the Haus der Ministerien. Yes, there they went, not so gay and laughing now. Tired perhaps. And now here she came, less lively, but still with that beautiful careless stride. Bond watched the blown golden hair and the fawn raincoat until it had vanished into the indigo dusk up the Wilhemstrasse. Where did she live? In some miserable flaked room in the suburbs? Or in one of the privileged apartments in the hideous lavatory-tiled Stalinallee?

Bond drew himself back. Somewhere, within easy reach, that girl lived. Was she married? Did she have a lover? Anyway, to hell with it! She was not for him.

The next day, and the next night watch, were duplicates, with small variations, of the first. James Bond had his two more brief rendezvous, by sniperscope, with the girl, and the rest was a killing of time and a tightening of the tension that, by the time the third and final day came, was like a fog in the small room.

James Bond crammed the third day with an almost lunatic program of museums, art galleries, the zoo, and a film, hardly perceiving anything he looked at, his mind's eye divided between the girl and those four black squares and the black tube and the unknown man behind it—the man he was now certainly going to kill tonight.

Back punctually at five in the apartment, Bond narrowly averted a row with Captain Sender because, that evening, Bond took a stiff drink of the whiskey before he donned the hideous cowl that now stank of his sweat. Captain Sender had tried to prevent him, and when he failed, had threatened to call up Head of Station and report Bond for breaking training.

"Look, my friend," said Bond wearily, "I've got to commit a murder tonight. Not you. Me. So be a good chap and stuff it, would you? You can tell Tanqueray anything you like when it's over. Think I like this job? Having a Double-O number and so on? I'd be quite happy for you to get me sacked from the Double-O Section. Then I could settle down and make a snug nest of papers as an ordinary staffer. Right?" Bond drank down his whiskey, reached for his thriller—now arriving at an appalling climax— and threw himself on the bed.

Captain Sender, icily silent, went off into the kitchen to brew, from the sounds, his inevitable cuppa.

Bond felt the whiskey beginning to melt the coiled nerves in his stomach. Now then, Liselotte, how in hell are you going to get out of this fix?

It was exactly six-five when Sender, at his post, began talking excitedly. "Bond, there's something moving way back over there. Now he's stopped—wait, no, he's on the move again, keeping low. There's a bit of broken wall there. He'll be out of sight of the opposition. But thick weeds, yards of them, ahead of him. Christ! He's coming through the weeds. And they're moving. Hope to God they think it's only the wind. Now he's through and gone to ground. Any reaction?"

"No," said Bond tensely. "Keep on telling me. How far to the frontier?"

"He's only got about fifty yards to go," Captain Sender's voice was harsh with excitement. "Broken stuff, but some of it's open. Then a solid chunk of wall right up against the pavement. He'll have to get over it. They can't fail to spot him then. Now! Now he's made ten yards, and another ten. Got him clearly then. Blackened his face and hands. Get ready! Any moment now he'll make the last sprint."

James Bond felt the sweat pouring down his face and neck. He took a chance and quickly wiped his hands down his sides and then got them back to the rifle, his finger inside the guard, just lying along

the curved trigger. "There's something moving in the room behind the gun. They must have spotted him. Get that Opel working."

Bond heard the code word go into the microphone, heard the Opel in the street below start up, felt his pulse quicken as the engine leaped into life and a series of ear-splitting cracks came from the exhaust.

The movement in the black cave was now definite. A black arm with a black glove had reached out and under the stock.

"Now!" called out Captain Sender. "Now! He's run for the wall! He's up it! Just going to jump!"

And then, in the sniperscope, Bond saw the head of Trigger—the purity of the profile, the golden bell of hair—all laid out along the stock of the Kalashnikov! She was dead, a sitting duck! Bond's fingers flashed down to the screws, inched them round, and as yellow flame fluttered at the snout of the submachinegun, squeezed the trigger.

The bullet, dead-on at three hundred and ten yards, must have hit where the stock ended up the barrel, might have got her in the left hand—but the effect was to tear the gun off its mountings, smash it against the side of the window frame, and then hurl it out of the window. It turned several times on its way down and crashed into the middle of the street.

"He's over!" shouted Captain Sender. "He's over! He's done it! My God, he's done it!"

"Get down!" said Bond sharply, and threw himself sideways off the bed as the big eye of a searchlight in one of the black windows blazed on, swerving up the street toward their block and their room. Then gunfire crashed, and the bullets howled into their window, ripping the curtains, smashing the woodwork, thudding into the walls.

Behind the roar and zing of the bullets, Bond heard the Opel race off down the street, and, behind that again, the fragmentary whisper of the orchestra. The combination of the two background noises clicked. Of course! The orchestra, that must have raised an infernal din throughout the offices and corridors of the Haus der Ministerien, was, as on their side the back-firing Opel, designed to provide some cover for the sharp burst of fire from Trigger. Had she carried her weapon to and fro every day in that cello case? Was the whole orchestra composed of KGB women? Had the other instrument cases contained only equipment—the big drum perhaps the searchlight—while the real instruments were available in the concert hall? Too elaborate? Too fantastic? Probably.

But there had been no doubt about the girl. In the sniperscope, Bond had even been able to see one wide, heavily lashed, aiming eye. Had he hurt her? Almost certainly her left arm. There would be no chance of seeing her, seeing how she was, if she left with the orchestra. Now he would never see her again. Bond's window would be a death trap. To underline the fact, a stray bullet smashed into the mechanism of the Winchester, already overturned and damaged, and hot lead splashed down on Bond's hand, burning the skin. On Bond's emphatic oath, the firing stopped abruptly and silence sang in the room.

Captain Sender emerged from beside his bed, brushing glass out of his hair. Bond and Sender crunched across the floor and through the splintered door into the kitchen. Here, because the room faced away from the street, it was safe to switch on the light.

"Any damage?" asked Bond.

"No. You all right?" Captain Sender's pale eyes were bright with the fever that comes in battle. They also, Bond noticed, held a sharp glint of accusation.

"Yes. Just get an Elastoplast for my hand. Caught a splash from one of the bullets." Bond went into the bathroom. When he came out, Captain Sender was sitting by the walkie-talkie he had fetched from the sitting room. He was speaking into it. Now he said into the microphone, "That's all for now. Fine about 272. Hurry the armored car, if you would. Be glad to get out of here, and 007 will need to write his version of what happened. Okay? Then *over* and *out*."

Captain Sender turned to Bond. Half accusing, half embarrassed he said, "Afraid Head of Station needs your reasons in writing for not getting that chap. I had to tell him I'd seen you alter your aim at the last second. Gave Trigger time to get off a burst. Damned lucky for 272 he'd just begun his sprint. Blew chunks off the wall behind him. What was it all about?"

James Bond knew he could lie, knew he could fake a dozen reasons why. Instead he took a deep pull at the strong whiskey he had poured for himself, put the glass down, and looked Captain Sender straight in the eye.

"Trigger was a woman."

"So what? KGB has got plenty of women agents—and women gunners. I'm not in the least surprised. The Russian woman's team always does well in the World Championships. Last meeting, in Moscow, they came first, second, and third against seventeen countries. I can even remember two of their names—

Donskaya and Lomova. Terrific shots. She may even have been one of them. What did she look like? Records'll probably be able to turn her up."

"She was a blonde. She was the girl who carried the cello in that orchestra. Probably had her gun in the cello case. The orchestra was to cover up the shooting."

"Oh!" said Captain Sender slowly. "I see. The girl you were keen on?"

"That's right."

"Well, I'm sorry, but I'll have to put that in my report too. You had clear orders to exterminate Trigger."

There came the sound of a car approaching. It pulled up somewhere below. The bell rang twice. Sender said, "Well, let's get going. They've sent an armored car to get us out of here." He paused. His eyes flicked over Bond's shoulder, avoiding Bond's eyes. "Sorry about the report. Got to do my duty, y'know. You should have killed that sniper whoever it was."

Bond got up. He suddenly didn't want to leave the stinking little smashed-up flat, leave the place from which, for three days, he had had this long-range, one-sided romance with an unknown girl—an unknown enemy agent with much the same job in her outfit as he had in his. Poor little bitch! She would be in worse trouble now than he was! She'd certainly be court-martialed for muffing this job. Probably be kicked out of the KGB. He shrugged. At least they'd stop short of killing her—as he himself had done.

James Bond said wearily, "Okay. With any luck it'll cost me my Double-O number. But tell Head of

Station not to worry. That girl won't do any more sniping. Probably lost her left hand. Certainly broke her nerve for that kind of work. Scared the living daylights out of her. In my book, that was enough. Let's go."

THE PROPERTY OF A LADY

It was, exceptionally, a hot day in early June. James Bond put down the dark gray chalk pencil that was the marker for the dockets routed to the Double-O Section and took off his coat. He didn't bother to hang it over the back of his chair, let alone take the trouble to get up and drape the coat over the hanger Mary Goodnight had suspended, at her own cost (damn women!), behind the Office of Works' green door of his connecting office. He dropped the coat on the floor. There was no reason to keep the coat immaculate, the creases tidy. There was no sign of any work to be done. All over the world there was quiet. The In and Out signals had, for weeks, been routine. The daily top secret SITREP, even the newspapers, yawned vacuously—in the latter case scratchings at domestic scandals for readership, for bad news, the only news that makes such sheets readable, whether top secret or on sale for pennies.

Bond hated these periods of vacuum. His eyes, his mind, were barely in focus as he turned the pages of a jaw-breaking dissertation by the Scientific Research Station on the Russian use of cyanide gas, propelled by the cheapest bulb-handled children's water pistol, for assassination. The spray, it seemed, directed at the face, took instantaneous effect. It was recommended for victims from 25 years upwards, on ascending stairways or inclines. The verdict would then probably be heart-failure.

The harsh burr of the red telephone sprayed into the room so suddenly that James Bond, his mind elsewhere, reached his hand automatically towards his left armpit in self-defense. The edges of his mouth turned down as he recognized the reflex. On the second burr he picked up the receiver.

"Sir?"

"Sir."

He got up from his chair and picked up his coat. He put on the coat and at the same time put on his mind. He had been dozing in his bunk. Now he had to go up on the bridge. He walked through into the connecting office and resisted the impulse to ruffle up the inviting nape of Mary Goodnight's golden neck.

He told her "M." and walked out into the close-carpeted corridor and along, between the muted whizz and zing of the Communications Section, of which his Section was a neighbor, to the lift and up to the eighth.

Miss Moneypenny's expression conveyed nothing. It usually conveyed something if she knew something—private excitement, curiosity, or, if Bond was in trouble, encouragement or even anger. Now the smile of welcome showed disinterest. Bond registered that this was going to be some kind of a routine job, a bore, and he adjusted his entrance through that fateful door accordingly.

There was a visitor—a stranger. He sat on M.'s left. He only briefly glanced up as Bond came in and took his usual place across the red-leather-topped desk.

M. said, stiffly, "Dr. Fanshawe, I don't think you've met Commander Bond of my Research Department."

Bond was used to these euphemisms.

He got up and held out his hand. Dr. Fanshawe rose, briefly touched Bond's hand and sat quickly down as if he had touched paws with a Gila monster.

If he looked at Bond, inspected him and took him in as anything more than an anatomical silhouette, Bond thought that Dr. Fanshawe's eyes must be fitted with a thousandth of a second shutter. So this was obviously some kind of an expert—a man whose interests lay in facts, things, theories—not in human beings. Bond wished that M. had given him some kind of a brief, hadn't got this puckish, rather childishly malign desire to surprise—to spring the jack-in-a-box on his staff. But Bond, remembering his own boredom of ten minutes ago, and putting himself in M.'s place, had the intuition to realize that M. himself might have been subject to the same June heat, the same oppressive vacuum in his duties, and, faced by the unexpected relief of an emergency, a small one perhaps, had decided to extract the maximum effect, the maximum drama, out of it to relieve his own tedium.

The stranger was middle-aged, rosy, well-fed, and clothed rather foppishly in the neo-Edwardian fashion —turned-up cuffs to his dark blue, four-buttoned coat, a pearl pin in a heavy silk cravat, spotless wing collar,

cufflinks formed of what appeared to be antique coins,
pince-nez on a thick black ribbon. Bond summed him
up as something literary, a critic perhaps, a bachelor—
possibly with homosexual tendencies.

M. said, "Dr. Fanshawe is a noted authority on
antique jewelry. He is also, though this is confidential,
adviser to H.M. Customs and to the C.I.D. on such
things. He has in fact been referred to me by our
friends at M.I.5. It is in connection with our Miss
Freudenstein."

Bond raised his eyebrows. Maria Freudenstein was
a secret agent working for the Soviet KGB in the heart
of the Secret Service. She was in the Communications
Department, but in a watertight compartment of it that
had been created especially for her, and her duties
were confined to operating the Purple Cipher—a
cipher which had also been created especially for her.
Six times a day she was responsible for encoding and
dispatching lengthy SITREPS in this cipher to the
C.I.A. in Washington. These messages were the output of Section 100 which was responsible for running
double agents. They were an ingenious mixture of true
fact, harmless disclosures and an occasional nugget of
the grossest misinformation. Maria Freudenstein, who
had been known to be a Soviet agent when she was
taken into the Service, had been allowed to steal the
key to the Purple Cipher with the intention that the
Russians should have complete access to these
SITREPS—be able to intercept and decipher them—
and thus, when appropriate, be fed false information.
It was a highly secret operation which needed to be
handled with extreme delicacy, but it had now been
running smoothly for three years and, if Maria Freu-

denstein also picked up a certain amount of canteen gossip at Headquarters, that was a necessary risk, and she was not attractive enough to form liaisons which could be a security risk.

M. turned to Dr. Fanshawe. "Perhaps, Doctor, you would care to tell Commander Bond what it is all about."

"Certainly, certainly." Dr. Fanshawe looked quickly at Bond and then away again. He addressed his boots. "You see, it's like this, er, Commander. You've heard of a man called Fabergé, no doubt. Famous Russian jeweler."

"Made fabulous Easter eggs for the Czar and Czarina before the revolution."

"That was indeed one of his specialties. He made many other exquisite pieces of what we may broadly describe as objects of vertu. Today, in the sale rooms, the best examples fetch truly fabulous prices—£50,000 and more. And recently there entered this country the most amazing specimen of all—the so-called Emerald Sphere, a work of supreme art hitherto known only from a sketch by the great man himself. This treasure arrived by registered post from Paris and it was addressed to this woman of whom you know, Miss Maria Freudenstein."

"Nice little present. Might I ask how you learned of it, Doctor?"

"I am, as your Chief has told you, an adviser to H.M. Customs and Excise in matters concerning antique jewelry and similar works of art. The declared value of the package was £100,000. This was unusual. There are methods of opening such packages clandestinely. The package was opened—under a

Home Office Warrant, of course—and I was called in
to examine the contents and give a valuation. I im-
mediately recognized the Emerald Sphere from the
account and sketch of it given in Mr. Kenneth Snowman's definitive work on Fabergé. I said that the
declared price might well be on the low side. But
what I found of particular interest was the accom-
panying document which gave, in Russian and French,
the provenance of this priceless object." Dr. Fanshawe
gestured towards a photostat of what appeared to be
a brief family tree that lay on the desk in front of
M. "That is a copy I had made. Briefly, it states that
the Sphere was commissioned by Miss Freudenstein's
grandfather directly from Fabergé in 1917—no doubt
as a means of turning some of his rubles into something portable and of great value. On his death in
1918 it passed to his brother and thence, in 1950, to
Miss Freudenstein's mother. She, it appears, left Russia
as a child and lived in White Russian émigré circles
in Paris. She never married, but gave birth to this
girl, Maria, illegitimately. It seems that she died last
year and that some friend or executor, the paper is
not signed, has now forwarded the Sphere to its right-
ful owner, Miss Maria Freudenstein. I had no reason
to question this girl, although as you can imagine my
interest was most lively, until last month Sotheby's
announced that they would auction the piece, described
as 'the property of a lady' in a week from today. On
behalf of the British Museum and, er, other interested
parties, I then made discreet inquiries and met the
lady, who, with perfect composure, confirmed the
rather unlikely story contained in the provenance. It
was then that I learned that she worked for the Min-

istry of Defense and it crossed my rather suspicious mind that it was, to say the least of it, odd that a junior clerk, engaged presumably on sensitive duties, should suddenly receive a gift to the value of £100,-000 or more from abroad. I spoke to a senior official in M.I.5 with whom I have some contact through my work for H.M. Customs and I was in due course referred to this, er, department." Dr. Fanshawe spread his hands and gave Bond a brief glance. "And that, Commander, is all I have to tell you."

M. broke in, "Thank you, Doctor. Just one or two final questions and I won't detain you any further. You have examined this emerald ball thing and you pronounce it genuine?"

Dr. Fanshawe ceased gazing at his boots. He looked up and spoke to a point somewhere above M.'s left shoulder. "Certainly. So does Mr. Snowman of Wartski's, the greatest Fabergé experts and dealers in the world. It is undoubtedly the missing masterpiece of which hitherto Carl Fabergé's sketch was the only record."

"What about the provenance? What do the experts say about that?"

"It stands up adequately. The greatest Fabergé pieces were nearly always privately commissioned. Miss Freudenstein says that her grandfather was a vastly rich man before the revolution—a porcelain manufacturer. Ninety-nine percent of all Fabergé's output has found its way abroad. There are only a few pieces left in the Kremlin—described simply as 'pre-revolutionary examples of Russian jewelry.' The official Soviet view has always been that they are merely capitalist baubles. Officially they despise them as they officially despise their superb collection of French Impressionists."

"So the Soviet still retain some examples of the work of this man Fabergé. Is it possible that this emerald affair could have lain secreted somewhere in the Kremlin through all these years?"

"Certainly. The Kremlin treasure is vast. No one knows what they keep hidden. They have only recently put on display what they have wanted to put on display."

M. drew on his pipe. His eyes through the smoke were bland, scarcely interested. "So that, in theory, there is no reason why this emerald ball should not have been unearthed from the Kremlin, furnished with a faked history to establish ownership, and transferred abroad as a reward to some friend of Russia for services rendered?"

"None at all. It would be an ingenious method of greatly rewarding the beneficiary without the danger of paying large sums into his, or her, bank account."

"But the final monetary reward would of course depend on the amount realized by the sale of the object—the auction price for instance?"

"Exactly."

"And what do you expect this object to fetch at Sotheby's?"

"Impossible to say. Wartski's will certainly bid very high. But of course they wouldn't be prepared to tell anyone just how high—either on their own account for stock, so to speak, or acting on behalf of a customer. Much would depend on how high they are forced up by an underbidder. Anyway, not less than £100,000 I'd say."

"Hm." M.'s mouth turned down at the corners. "Expensive hunk of jewelry."

Dr. Fanshawe was aghast at this barefaced revelation of M.'s philistinism. He actually looked M. straight in the face. "My dear sir," he expostulated, "do you consider the stolen Goya, sold at Sotheby's for £140,000, that went to the National Gallery, just an expensive hunk, as you put it, of canvas and paint?"

M. said placatingly, "Forgive me, Dr. Fanshawe. I expressed myself clumsily. I have never had the leisure to interest myself in works of art nor, on a naval officer's pay, the money to acquire any. I was just registering my dismay at the runaway prices being fetched at auction these days."

"You are entitled to your views, sir," said Dr. Fanshawe stuffily.

Bond thought it was time to rescue M. He also wanted to get Dr. Fanshawe out of the room so that they could get down to the professional aspects of this odd business. He got to his feet. He said to M., "Well, sir, I don't think there is anything else I need to know. No doubt this will turn out to be perfectly straightforward (like hell it would!) and just a matter of one of your staff turning out to be a very lucky woman. But it's very kind of Dr. Fanshawe to have gone to so much trouble." He turned to Dr. Fanshawe. "Would you care to have a staff car to take you wherever you're going?"

"No thank you, thank you very much. It will be pleasant to walk across the park."

Hands were shaken, good-byes said and Bond showed the doctor out. Bond came back into the room. M. had taken a bulky file, stamped with the top secret red star, out of a drawer and was already immersed in it. Bond took his seat again and waited. The room was silent save for the riffling of paper. This also stopped as M. extracted a foolscap sheet of blue cardboard used for Confidential Staff Records and carefully read through the forest of close type on both sides.

Finally he slipped it back in the file and looked up. "Yes," he said and the blue eyes were bright with interest. "It fits all right. The girl was born in Paris in 1935. Mother very active in the Resistance during the war. Helped run the Tulip Escape Route and got away with it. After the war, the girl went to the Sorbonne and then got a job in the Embassy, in the Naval Attaché's office, as an interpreter. You know the rest. She was compromised—some unattractive sexual business—by some of her mother's old Resistance friends who by then were working for the NKVD, and from then on she has been working under Control. She applied, no doubt on instruction, for British citizenship. Her clearance from the Embassy and her mother's Resistance record helped her to get that by 1959, and she was then recommended to us by the FO. But it was there that she made her big mistake. She asked for a year's leave before coming to us and was next reported by the Hutchinson network in the Leningrad espionage school. There she presumably received the usual training and we had to decide what to do about her. Section 100 thought up the Purple Cipher operation and you know the rest. She's been working for three years inside headquarters for the KGB and now she's getting her reward—this emerald ball thing worth

£100,000. And that's interesting on two counts. First it means that the KGB is totally hooked on the Purple Cipher or they wouldn't be making this fantastic payment. That's good news. It means that we can hot up the material we're passing over—put across some Grade 3 deception material and perhaps even move up to Grade 2. Secondly, it explains something we've never been able to understand—that this girl hasn't hitherto received a single payment for her services. We were worried by that. She had an account at Glyn, Mills that only registered her monthly paycheck of around £50. And she's consistently lived within it. Now she's getting her payoff in one large lump sum via this bauble we've been learning about. All very satisfactory."

M. reached for the ashtray made out of a twelve-inch shell base and rapped out his pipe with the air of a man who has done a good afternoon's work.

Bond shifted in his chair. He badly needed a cigarette, but he wouldn't have dreamed of lighting one. He wanted one to help him focus his thoughts. He felt that there were some ragged edges to this problem—one particularly. He said, mildly, "Have we ever caught up with her local Control, sir? How does she get her instructions?"

"Doesn't need to," said M. impatiently, busying himself with his pipe. "Once she'd got hold of the Purple Cipher all she needed to do was hold down her job. Damn it man, she's pouring the stuff into their lap six times a day. What sort of instructions would they need to give her? I doubt if the KGB men in London even know of her existence—perhaps the Resident Director does, but as you know we don't even know who he is. Give my eyes to find out."

Bond suddenly had a flash of intuition. It was as if a camera had started grinding in his skull, grinding out a length of clear film. He said quietly, "It might be that this business at Sotheby's could show him to us—show us who he is."

"What the devil are you talking about, 007? Explain yourself."

"Well sir," Bond's voice was calm with certainty, "you remember what this Dr. Fanshawe said about an underbidder—someone to make these Wartski merchants go to their very top price. If the Russians don't seem to know or care very much about Fabergé, as Dr. Fanshawe says, they may have no very clear idea what this thing's really worth. The KGB wouldn't be likely to know about such things anyway. They may imagine it's only worth its break-up value—say ten or twenty thousand pounds for the emerald. That sort of sum would make more sense than the small fortune the girl's going to get if Dr. Fanshawe's right. Well, if the Resident Director is the only man who knows about this girl, he will be the only man who knows she's been paid. So he'll be the underbidder. He'll be sent to Sotheby's and told to push the sale through the roof. I'm certain of it. So we'll be able to identify him and we'll have enough on him to have him sent home. He just won't know what's hit him. Nor will the KGB. If I can go to the sale and bowl him out and we've got the place covered with cameras, and the auction records, we can get the FO to declare him persona non grata inside a week. And Resident Directors don't grow on trees. It may be months before the KGB can appoint a replacement."

M. said, thoughtfully, "Perhaps you've got something there." He swiveled his chair round and gazed out of the big window towards the jagged skyline of London. Finally he said, over his shoulder, "All right, 007. Go and see the Chief of Staff and set the machinery up. I'll square things with Five. It's their territory, but it's our bird. There won't be any trouble. But don't go and get carried away and bid for this bit of rubbish yourself. I haven't got the money to spare."

Bond said, "No sir." He got to his feet and went quickly out of the room. He thought he had been very clever and he wanted to see if he had. He didn't want M. to change his mind.

Wartski has a modest, ultra-modern frontage at 138 Regent Street. The window, with a restrained show of modern and antique jewelry, gave no hint that these were the greatest Fabergé-dealers in the world. The interior—gray carpet, walls paneled in sycamore, a few unpretentious vitrines—held none of the excitement of Cartier's, Boucheron or Van Cleef, but the group of famed Royal Warrants from Queen Mary, the Queen Mother, the Queen, King Paul of Greece and the unlikely King Frederick IX of Denmark, suggested that this was no ordinary jeweler.

James Bond asked for Mr. Kenneth Snowman. A good-looking, very well-dressed man of about 40 rose from a group of men sitting with their heads together at the back of the room and came forward.

Bond said quietly, "I'm from the C.I.D. Can we

have a talk? Perhaps you'd like to check my credentials first. My name's James Bond. But you'll have to go direct to Sir Ronald Vallance or his P.A. I'm not directly on the strength at Scotland Yard. Sort of liaison job."

The intelligent, observant eyes didn't appear even to look him over. The man smiled. "Come on downstairs. Just having a talk with some American friends—sort of correspondents really. From 'Old Russia' on Fifth Avenue."

"I know the place," said Bond. "Full of rich-looking icons and so on. Not far from the Pierre."

"That's right." Mr. Snowman seemed even more reassured. He led the way down a narrow, thickly carpeted stairway into a large and glittering showroom which was obviously the real treasure house of the shop. Gold and diamonds and cut stones winked from lit cases round the walls.

"Have a seat. Cigarette?"

Bond took one of his own. "It's about this Fabergé that's coming up at Sotheby's tomorrow—this Emerald Sphere."

"Ah, yes." Mr. Snowman's clear brow furrowed anxiously. "No trouble about it I hope?"

"Not from your point of view. But we're very interested in the actual sale. We know about the owner, Miss Freudenstein. We think there may be an attempt to raise the bidding artificially. We're interested in the underbidder—assuming, that is, that your firm will be leading the field, so to speak."

"Well, er, yes," said Mr. Snowman with rather careful candor. "We're certainly going to go after it. But it'll sell for a huge price. Between you and me, we believe the V and A are going to bid, and probably the Metropolitan. But is it some crook you're after? If so you needn't worry. This is out of their class."

Bond said, "No. We're not looking for a crook." He wondered how far to go with this man. Because people are very careful with the secrets of their own business doesn't mean that they'll be careful with the secrets of yours. Bond picked up a wood and ivory plaque that lay on the table. It said:

> It is naught, it is naught, saith the buyer.
> But when he is gone his way, he boasteth.
> > Proverbs XX, 14

Bond was amused. He said so. "You can read the whole history of the bazaar, of the dealer and the customer, behind that quotation," he said. He looked Mr. Snowman straight in the eyes. "I need that sort of nose, that sort of intuition in this case. Will you give me a hand?"

"Certainly. If you'll tell me how I can help." He waved a hand. "If it's secrets you're worried about, please don't worry. Jewelers are used to them. Scotland Yard will probably give my firm a clean bill in that respect. Heaven knows we've had enough to do with them over the years."

"And if I told you that I'm from the Ministry of Defense?"

"Same thing," said Mr. Snowman. "You can naturally rely absolutely on my discretion!"

Bond made up his mind. "All right. Well, all this comes under the Official Secrets Act, of course. We suspect that the underbidder, presumably to you, will be a Soviet Agent. My job is to establish his identity. Can't tell you any more, I'm afraid. And you don't actually need to know any more. All I want is to go with you to Sotheby's tomorrow night and for you to help me spot the man. No medals, I'm afraid, but we'd be extremely grateful."

Mr. Kenneth Snowman's eyes glinted with enthusiasm. "Of course. Delighted to help in any way. But," he looked doubtful, "you know it's not necessarily going to be all that easy. Peter Wilson, the head of Sotheby's, who'll be taking the sale, would be the only person who could tell us for sure—that is, if the bidder wants to stay secret. There are dozens of ways of bidding without making any movement at all. But if the bidder fixes his method, his code so to speak, with Peter Wilson before the sale, Peter wouldn't think of letting anyone in on the code. It would give the bidder's game away to reveal his limit. And that's a close secret, as you can imagine, in the rooms. And a thousand times not if you come with me. I shall probably be setting the pace. I already know how far I'm going to go—for a client by the way—but it would make my job vastly easier if I could tell how far the underbidder's going to go. As it is, what you've told me has been a great help. I shall warn my man to put his sights even higher. If this chap of yours has got a strong nerve, he may push me very hard indeed. And there will be others in the field of course. It sounds as if this is going to be quite a night. They're putting it on television and asking all the millionaires and dukes and duchesses for the sort of gala performance Sotheby's do rather well. Wonderful publicity of course. By jove, if they knew there was cloak-and-dagger stuff mixed up with the sale, there'd be a riot! Now then, is there anything else to go into? Just spot this man and that's all?"

"That's all. How much do you think this thing will go for?"

Mr. Snowman tapped his teeth with a gold pencil. "Well now, you see that's where I have to keep quiet. I know how high I'm going to go, but that's my client's secret." He paused and looked thoughtful. "Let's say that if it goes for less than £100,000 we'll be surprised."

"I see," said Bond. "Now then, how do I get into the sale?"

Mr. Snowman produced an elegant alligator-skin notecase and extracted two engraved bits of pasteboard. He handed one over. "That's my wife's. I'll get her one somewhere else in the rooms. B.5—well placed in the center front. I'm B.6."

Bond took the ticket. It said:

Sotheby & Co.
Sale of
A Casket of Magnificent Jewels
and
A Unique Object of Vertu by Carl Fabergé
The Property of a Lady
Admit one to the Main Sale Room
Tuesday, 20 June, at 9.30 pm precisely
ENTRANCE IN ST. GEORGE STREET

"It's not the old Georgian entrance in Bond Street," commented Mr. Snowman. "They have an awning and red carpet out from their back door now that Bond

Street's one way. Now," he got up from his chair, "would you care to see some Fabergé? We've got some pieces here my father bought from the Kremlin around 1927. It'll give you some idea what all the fuss is about, though of course the Emerald Sphere's incomparably finer than anything I can show you by Fabergé apart from the Imperial Easter Eggs."

Later, dazzled by the diamonds, the multicolored gold, the silken sheen of translucent enamels, James Bond walked up and out of the Aladdin's Cave under Regent Street and went off to spend the rest of the day in drab offices around Whitehall planning drearily minute arrangements for the identification and photographing of a man in a crowded room who did not yet possess a face or an identity but who was certainly the top Soviet spy in London.

Through the next day, Bond's excitement mounted. He found an excuse to go into the Communications Section and wander into the little room where Miss Maria Freudenstein and two assistants were working the cipher machines that handled the Purple Cipher dispatches. He picked up the *en clair* file—he had freedom of access to most material at headquarters—and ran his eye down the carefully edited paragraphs that, in half an hour to so, would be spiked, unread, by some junior C.I.A. clerk in Washington and, in Moscow, be handed, with reverence, to a top-ranking officer of the KGB. He joked with the two junior girls, but Maria Freudenstein only looked up from her machine to give him a polite smile and Bond's skin crawled minutely at this proximity to treachery and at the black and deadly secret locked up beneath the frilly white blouse. She was an unattractive girl with a pale, rather pimply skin, black hair and a vaguely unwashed appearance. Such a girl would be unloved, make few friends, have chips on her shoulder—more particularly in view of her illegitimacy—and a grouse against society. Perhaps her only pleasure in life was the triumphant secret she harbored in that flattish bosom—the knowledge that she was cleverer than all those around her, that she was, every day, hitting back against the world—the world that despised, or just ignored her, because of her plainness—with all her might. One day they'd be sorry! It was a common neurotic pattern—the revenge of the ugly duckling on society.

Bond wandered off down the corridor to his own office. By tonight that girl would have made a fortune, been paid her thirty pieces of silver a thousandfold. Perhaps the money would change her character, bring her happiness. She would be able to afford the best beauty specialists, the best clothes, a pretty flat. But M. had said he was now going to hot up the Purple Cipher Operation, try a more dangerous level of deception. This would be dicey work. One false step, one incautious lie, an ascertainable falsehood in a message, and the KGB would smell a rat. Once more, and they would know they were being hoaxed and probably had been ignominiously hoaxed for three years. Such a shameful revelation would bring quick revenge. It would be assumed that Maria Freudenstein had been acting as a double agent, working for the British as well as the Russians. She would inevitably and quickly

be liquidated—perhaps with the cyanide pistol Bond
had been reading about only the day before.

James Bond, looking out of the window across the
trees in Regent's Park, shrugged. Thank God it was
none of his business. The girl's fate wasn't in his hands.
She was caught in the grimy machine of espionage and
she would be lucky if she lived to spend a tenth of
the fortune she was going to gain in a few hours in
the auction rooms.

There was a line of cars and taxis blocking George
Street behind Sotheby's. Bond paid off his taxi and
joined the crowd filtering under the awning and up
the steps. He was handed a catalog by the uniformed
Commissionaire who inspected his ticket, and went
up the broad stairs with the fashionable, excited
crowd and along a gallery and into the main auction
room that was already thronged. He found his seat
next to Mr. Snowman, who was writing figures on a
pad on his knee, and looked round him.

The lofty room was perhaps as large as a tennis
court. It had the look and the smell of age and the two
large chandeliers, to fit in with the period, blazed
warmly in contrast to the strip lighting along the
vaulted ceiling whose glass roof was partly obscured
by a blind, still half-drawn against the sun that would
have been blazing down on the afternoon's sale.
Miscellaneous pictures and tapestries hung on the
olive-green walls and batteries of television and other
cameras (amongst them the M.I.5 cameraman with
a press pass from *The Sunday Times*) were clustered
with their handlers on a platform built out from the

middle of a giant tapestried hunting scene. There were perhaps a hundred dealers and spectators sitting attentively on small gilt chairs. All eyes were focused on the slim, good-looking auctioneer talking quietly from the raised wooden pulpit. He was dressed in an immaculate dinner jacket with a red carnation in the buttonhole. He spoke unemphatically and without gestures.

"Fifteen thousand pounds. And sixteen," a pause. A glance at someone in the front row. "Against you, sir." The flick of a catalog being raised. "Seventeen thousand pounds I am bid. Eighteen. Nineteen. I am bid twenty thousand pounds." And so the quiet voice went, calmly, unhurriedly on while down among the audience the equally impassive bidders signaled their responses to the litany.

"What is he selling?" asked Bond opening his catalog.

"Lot 40," said Mr. Snowman. "That diamond rivière the porter's holding on the black velvet tray. It'll probably go for about twenty-five. An Italian is bidding against a couple of Frenchmen. Otherwise they'd have got it for twenty. I only went to fifteen. Liked to have got it. Wonderful stones. But there it is."

Sure enough, the price stuck at twenty-five thousand and the hammer, held by its head and not by its handle, came down with soft authority. "Yours, sir," said Mr. Peter Wilson and a sales clerk hurried down the aisle to confirm the identity of the bidder.

"I'm disappointed," said Bond.

Mr. Snowman looked up from his catalog. "Why is that?"

"I've never been to an auction before and I always

thought the auctioneer banged his gavel three times and said going, going, gone, so as to give the bidders a last chance."

Mr. Snowman laughed. "You might still find that operating in the Shires or in Ireland, but it hasn't been the fashion at London sale rooms since I've been attending them."

"Pity. It adds to the drama."

"You'll get plenty of that in a minute. This is the last lot before the curtain goes up."

One of the porters had reverently uncoiled a glittering mass of rubies and diamonds on his black velvet tray. Bond looked at the catalog. It said "Lot 41" which the luscious prose described as:

A PAIR OF FINE AND IMPORTANT RUBY AND DIAMOND BRACELETS, the front of each in the form of an elliptical cluster composed of one larger and two smaller rubies within a border of cushioned-shaped diamonds, the sides and back formed of simpler clusters alternating with diamond openwork scroll motifs springing from single-stone ruby centers millegriffe-set in gold, running between chains of rubies and diamonds linked alternately, the clasp also in the form of an elliptical cluster.

❖ According to family tradition, this lot was formerly the property of Mrs. Fitzherbert (1756-1837) whose marriage to The Prince of Wales afterwards Geo. IV was definitely established when in 1905 a sealed packet deposited at Coutts Bank in 1833 and opened by Royal permission disclosed the marriage certificate and other conclusive proofs.

These bracelets were probably given by Mrs. Fitzherbert to her niece, who was described by the Duke of Orleans as "the prettiest girl in England."

While the bidding progressed, Bond slipped out of his seat and went down the aisle to the back of the room where the overflow audience spread out into the New Gallery and the Entrance Hall to watch the sale on closed-circuit television. He casually inspected the crowd, seeking any face he could recognize from the 200 members of the Soviet embassy staff whose photographs, clandestinely obtained, he had been studying during the past days. But amidst an audience that defied classification—a mixture of dealers, amateur collectors and what could be broadly classified as rich pleasure-seekers—was not a feature, let alone a face, that he could recognize except from the gossip columns. One or two sallow faces might have been Russian, but equally they might have belonged to half a dozen European races. There was a scattering of dark glasses, but dark glasses are no longer a disguise. Bond went back to his seat. Presumably the man would have to divulge himself when the bidding began.

"Fourteen thousand I am bid. And fifteen. Fifteen thousand." The hammer came down. "Yours, sir."

There was a hum of excitement and a fluttering of catalogs. Mr. Snowman wiped his forehead with a white silk handkerchief. He turned to Bond. "Now I'm afraid you are more or less on your own. I've got to pay attention to the bidding and anyway for some unknown reason it's considered bad form to look over one's shoulder to see who's bidding against you—if you're in the trade that's to say—so I'll only be able to spot him if he's somewhere up front here, and I'm afraid that's unlikely. Pretty well all dealers, but you can stare around as much as you like. What you've got to do is to watch Peter Wilson's eyes and then try and see who he's looking at, or who's looking at him. If you can spot the man, which may be quite difficult, note any movement he makes, even the very smallest. Whatever the man does—scratching his head, pulling at the lobe of his ear or whatever, will be a code he's arranged with Peter Wilson. I'm afraid he won't do anything obvious like raising his catalog. Do you get me? And don't forget that he may make absolutely no movement at all until right at the end when he's pushed me as far as he thinks I'll go, then he'll want to sign off. Mark you," Mr. Snowman smiled, "when we get to the last lap I'll put plenty of heat on him and try and make him show his hand. That's assuming of course that we are the only two bidders left in." He looked enigmatic. "And I think you can take it that we shall be."

From the man's certainty, James Bond felt pretty sure that Mr. Snowman had been given instructions to get the Emerald Sphere at any cost.

A sudden hush fell as a tall pedestal draped in black velvet was brought in with ceremony and positioned in front of the auctioneer's rostrum. Then a handsome oval case of what looked like white velvet was placed on top of the pedestal and, with reverence, an elderly porter in gray uniform with wine-red sleeves, collar and back belt, unlocked it and lifted out Lot 42, placed it on the black velvet and removed the case. The cricket ball of polished emerald on its exquisite base glowed with a supernatural green fire and the jewels on its surface and on the opalescent meridian winked their various colors. There was a gasp of admiration from the audience and even the clerks and experts behind the rostrum and sitting at the tall counting-house desk beside the auctioneer, accustomed to the Crown jewels of Europe parading before their eyes, leaned forward to get a better look.

James Bond turned to his catalog. There it was, in heavy type and in prose as stickily luscious as a butter-scotch sundae:

THE TERRESTRIAL GLOBE

DESIGNED IN 1917 BY CARL FABERGÉ FOR A RUSSIAN GENTLEMAN AND NOW THE PROPERTY OF HIS GRANDDAUGHTER

42 A VERY IMPORTANT FABERGÉ TERRESTRIAL GLOBE. A sphere carved from an extraordinarily large piece of Siberian emerald matrix weighing approximately one thousand three hundred carats and of a superb color and vivid translucence, represents a terrestrial globe supported upon an elaborate *rocaille* scroll mount finely chased in *quatre-couleur* gold and set with a profusion of rose-diamonds and small emeralds of intense color, to form a table-clock.

Around this mount six gold *putti* disport themselves among cloud-forms which are naturalistically rendered in carved rock-crystal finished matt and veined with fine lines of tiny rose-diamonds.

The globe itself, the surface of which is meticulously engraved with a map of the world with the principal cities indicated by brilliant diamonds embedded within gold collets, rotates mechanically on an axis controlled by a small clock-movement, by *G. Moser*, signed, which is concealed in the base, and is girdled by a fixed gold belt enameled opalescent oyster along a reserved path in *champlevé* technique over a moiré *guillochage* with painted Roman numerals in pale sepia enamel serving as the dial of the clock, and a single triangular pigeon-blood Burma ruby of about five carats set into the surface of the orb, pointing the hour. Height: 7½ *in. Workmaster, Henrik Wigström.* In the original double-opening white velvet, satin-lined, oviform case with the gold key fitted in the base.

❖ The theme of this magnificent sphere is one that had inspired Fabergé some fifteen years earlier, as evidenced in the miniature terrestrial globe which forms part of the Royal Collection at Sandringham. (See plate 280 in *The Art of Carl Fabergé,* by A. Kenneth Snowman.)

After a brief and searching glance round the room, Mr. Wilson banged his hammer softly. "Lot 42—an object of vertu by Carl Fabergé." A pause. "Twenty thousand pounds I am bid."

Mr. Snowman whispered to Bond, "That means he's probably got a bid of at least fifty. This is simply to get things moving."

Catalogs fluttered. "And thirty, forty, fifty thousand pounds I am bid. And sixty, seventy, and eighty thousand pounds. And ninety." A pause and then: "One hundred thousand pounds I am bid."

There was a rattle of applause round the room. The cameras had swiveled to a youngish man, one of three on a raised platform to the left of the auctioneer who were speaking softly into telephones. Mr. Snowman commented, "That's one of Sotheby's young men. He'll be on an open line to America. I should think that's the Metropolitan bidding, but it might be anybody. Now it's time for me to get to work." Mr. Snowman flicked up his rolled catalog.

"And ten," said the auctioneer. The man spoke into his telephone and nodded. "And twenty."

Again a flick from Mr. Snowman.

"And thirty."

The man on the telephone seemed to be speaking rather more words than before into his mouthpiece— perhaps giving his estimate of how much further the price was likely to go. He gave a slight shake of his head in the direction of the auctioneer and Peter Wilson looked away from him and round the room.

"One hundred and thirty thousand pounds I am bid," he repeated quietly.

Mr. Snowman said, softly, to Bond, "Now you'd better watch out. America seems to have signed off. It's time for your man to start pushing me."

James Bond slid out of his place and went and stood amongst a group of reporters in a corner to the left of the rostrum. Peter Wilson's eyes were directed towards the far right-hand corner of the room. Bond could detect no movement, but the auctioneer an-

nounced "And forty thousand pounds." He looked
down at Mr. Snowman. After a long pause Mr. Snowman raised five fingers. Bond guessed that this was
part of his process of putting the heat on. He was
showing reluctance, hinting that he was near the end
of his tether.

"One hundred and forty-five thousand." Again the
piercing glance towards the back of the room. Again
no movement. But again some signal had been exchanged. "One hundred and fifty thousand pounds."

There was a buzz of comment and some desultory
clapping. This time Mr. Snowman's reaction was even
slower and the auctioneer twice repeated the last bid.
Finally he looked directly at Mr. Snowman. "Against
you, sir." At last Mr. Snowman raised five fingers.

"One hundred and fifty-five thousand pounds."

James Bond was beginning to sweat. He had got
absolutely nowhere and the bidding must surely be
coming to an end. The auctioneer repeated the bid.

And now there was the tiniest movement. At the
back of the room, a chunky-looking man in a dark suit
reached up and unobtrusively took off his dark glasses.
It was a smooth, nondescript face—the sort of face
that might belong to a bank manager, a member of
Lloyd's, or a doctor. This must have been the pre-
arranged code with the auctioneer. So long as the man
wore his dark glasses he would raise in tens of thou-
sands. When he took them off, he had quit.

Bond shot a quick glance towards the bank of
cameramen. Yes, the M.I.5 photographer was on his
toes. He had also seen the movement. He lifted his
camera deliberately and there was the quick glare of
a flash. Bond got back to his seat and whispered to

Snowman, "Got him. Be in touch with you tomorrow. Thanks a lot." Mr. Snowman only nodded. His eyes remained glued on the auctioneer.

Bond slipped out of his place and walked swiftly down the aisle as the auctioneer said for the third time, "One hundred and fifty-five thousand pounds I am bid," and then softly brought down his hammer. "Yours, sir."

Bond got to the back of the room before the audience had risen, applauding, to its feet. His quarry was hemmed in amongst the gilt chairs. He had now put on his dark glasses again and Bond put on a pair of his own. He contrived to slip into the crowd and get behind the man as the chattering crowd streamed down the stairs. The hair grew low down on the back of the man's rather squat neck and the lobes of his ears were pinched in close to his head. He had a slight hump, perhaps only a bone deformation, high up on his back. Bond suddenly remembered. This was Piotr Malinowski, with the official title on the Embassy staff of "Agricultural Attaché." So!

Outside, the man began walking swiftly towards Conduit Street. James Bond got unhurriedly into a taxi with its engine running and its flag down. He said to the driver, "That's him. Take it easy."

"Yes, sir," said the M.I.5 driver, pulling away from the curb.

The man picked up a taxi in Bond Street. The tail in the mixed evening traffic was easy. Bond's satisfaction mounted as the Russian's taxi turned up north of the Park and along Bayswater. It was just a question whether he would turn down the private entrance into Kensington Palace Gardens, where the first mansion on the left is the massive building of the Soviet Embassy. If he did, that would clinch matters. The two patrolling policemen, the usual Embassy guards, had been specially picked that night. It was their job just to confirm that the occupant of the leading taxi actually entered the Soviet Embassy.

Then, with the Secret Service evidence and the evidence of Bond and of the M.I.5 cameraman, there would be enough for the Foreign Office to declare Comrade Piotr Malinowski persona non grata on the grounds of espionage activity and send him packing. In the grim chess game that is secret service work, the Russians would have lost a queen. It would have been a very satisfactory visit to the auction rooms.

The leading taxi *did* turn in through the big iron gates.

Bond smiled with grim satisfaction. He leaned forward. "Thanks, driver. Headquarters please."